W9-BWU-952

Hero at Large
ROBYN AMOS

SILHOUETTE
SENSATION

Special thanks and acknowledgement are given
to Robyn Amos for her contribution.

*First published in Great Britain 2001
Large Print edition 2005
Silhouette Books Limited,
Eton House, 18-24 Paradise Road,
Richmond, Surrey, TW9 1SR*

© Harlequin Books S.A. 2000

ISBN 0 373 60241 3

*Set in Times Roman 18¼ on 20 pt.
34-0305-51083*

*Printed and bound in Great Britain
by Antony Rowe Ltd, Chippenham, Wiltshire*

Dear Reader,

Writing a story that takes place in LA was fun because the city nightlife is dramatically different from the nightlife of my own home city of Gaithersburg, Maryland. While writing this story, I also enjoyed tunnelling into the dark, shadowed life of an undercover government agent and rediscovering how the power of love can heal even the worst betrayals. These new elements were fun for me to explore, but there was one aspect of *Hero at Large* that was very familiar to me. Writing about a heroine who makes her living as a psychologist came naturally because I was once on the road to becoming one myself. After graduating from college with a degree in psychology, I decided that writing about the suspenseful and romantic lives of the people in my imagination was more fulfilling than writing research papers. I hope you enjoy *Hero at Large*.

Sincerely,

Robyn Amos

Prologue

Regrets were a waste of time. Keshon Gray had lived as a criminal long enough to know that much.

Stepping onto the rooftop, he took a pack of cigarettes out of his breast pocket. Gray only had a minute or two before he had to go back to the pretense of being a bouncer for L.A.'s trendy nightspot Ocean. But this time, as he struck a match and held it to the end of his cigarette, a strange sensation washed over him.

Before his break he'd helped move a

shipment of cocaine, but that wasn't what was pushing against the edges of his conscience. Nor was it the crates of semiautomatic Street Sweeper shotguns stacked in the storeroom beside the paper cups. He released a short puff, and as he watched the blue smoke curl and blend with the cool November air, it hit him.

Once he'd hated cigarettes…and smoking. At the back of his mind lived the memory of a time when he'd sworn the habit would never touch him.

Gray's first toke on a cigarette had been to prove himself to his boys. And even after he'd long outgrown that need, the habit remained, like sooty residue in the wake of a fire.

Each guise he'd taken on over the years—and there had been many—left a new layer of grime clinging to his soul. But he had no more choice now than he'd had thirteen years ago.

He may not have chosen the right path in life, but he'd done it for survival—not his own, someone else's. He'd made up his mind to do whatever he had to, but he hadn't been quick enough or strong enough then, and someone he'd loved like a brother had died.

Suddenly Gray's throat constricted and he felt as if he was choking. His cough was rough as he struggled to clear his throat, his eyes watering with the effort.

Even now, he couldn't think of that episode in his life with the numbing cool he was able to apply to everything else. For that reason, Gray had never failed again— at anything. He approached each new challenge as though someone's life depended upon his success—and more often than not, it did.

Since he'd returned to L.A., he'd reconnected with the remains of the gang he had belonged to. Those who weren't dead or in prison had been floundering on the edges of the L.A. drug trade and getting nowhere fast.

He herded them off street corners where they'd been hustling, and yanked them out of basements where they wasted their days getting high. It was time for them to move from petty street dealing into the big time. Making real money in this business required contacts, which he'd been cultivating carefully. Add a little weapons brokering into the mix, and they had an organized operation with the flashy L.A. club scene as the perfect cover.

The secret agency Gray worked for, SPEAR (Stealth, Perseverance, Endeavor, Attack and Rescue) was on the trail of a traitor—not a small problem since most government organizations didn't even know that SPEAR existed. Those that did know of SPEAR recognized them as a group of the most elite, well-trained operatives in the world. A fact that made this turncoat's threat to the agency all the more menacing.

He was willing to do whatever he had to do to bring down the enemy, but the fact was, he'd been hiding in shadows for so long, he no longer knew what he looked like in the light.

Gray stared at the cigarette burning between his fingers. Reflexively, he spread his index and middle finger and watched the cigarette fall over the edge of the roof and into the darkness below.

The time for mourning lost opportunities had passed. He'd made his choices and now he had to play them out. It didn't matter that he'd never based those choices on his own needs. Trying to find the man he'd lost so many years ago was pointless. In fact, that man had never existed. Gray had only been sixteen when his identity had begun to slip away.

He took a step back, straightening the collar on his black blazer, which he wore over jeans and a T-shirt, both black. His break was over. And so was the bitter-sweet glimpse of his past.

As Gray hurried down the stairs, he couldn't know that after nine years, he was about to look into the eyes of the only person who had ever known the real Keshon Gray.

Chapter 1

Even small victories deserved to be celebrated. Rennie Williams had been a psychologist long enough to appreciate that fact.

She smiled across the table at her two best friends. Their busy schedules had prevented them from having a girls' night out for quite a while, and now they were making up for lost time.

''We have a lot to celebrate tonight.'' As she reached for her margarita, Rennie's gaze shifted to the first person she'd met when she moved back to L.A.—a corporate attorney she'd picked out of the phone book to help her sort through the legal details of setting up a private practice. "To Marlena, the only woman to be made a partner at Loudon, Crosby and Wade."

Then Rennie turned to the second woman at the table, a nurse at the Family Planning Clinic, which was located in the L.A. Help Center on the same floor as Rennie's office. "To Alise, after two years with a man who didn't deserve you, you're finally free. And to me, for making it through my first year on my own as a counselor for women."

The women started to raise their glasses in salute, but Rennie held them off. "I'm almost done. To feminine energy, wisdom and strength," Rennie said, finishing her toast. "We've proven we can do anything."

Marlena and Alise cheered, clinking their glasses against hers.

The past year hadn't been easy for Rennie, but that only made her small successes more meaningful. Tonight one of her clients, Sarita Juarez, was making her singing debut in Ocean nightclub's Sand Castle Lounge, which featured salsa music. It was the perfect opportunity for Rennie to have a well-deserved good time with her friends and to show support for the client Rennie had struggled hardest to reach over the last few months.

When Rennie's mind drifted back from her reverie, she noticed that Alise and Marlena were having a spirited discussion on their favorite topic—men.

Marlena shot Rennie one of her world-famous probing looks. ''You're the shrink, Ren. Why are women so attracted to bad boys?''

Caught off guard, Rennie looked from

one woman to the other. "How did you two get onto *this* topic?"

Alise grinned. "Marlena has a theory that certain types of men are like irresistible poison. She thinks if we compare notes, we can come up with an antidote."

"Yeah. There must be some psychological concept to back my theory, right, Rennie?"

She took a long sip from her drink, enjoying the tangy lime taste. "I'm off the clock, guys. You're on your own." The spicy salsa tempo was working its way down her spine. She was having too much fun to get into a heavy discussion about men.

Marlena threw a twenty on the table. "There. That should cover fifteen minutes of your time. Go," she ordered, snapping her fingers.

Laughing, Rennie threw the money at her friend. Marlena was the type who expected to get her way and it was useless to fight it. "Fine. It's really not that complicated. A woman has an inherent need to tame the wild beast. We're attracted to bad boys because they're sexy and dangerous, and we secretly believe that we can change them."

"Yeah, but we all know that's a crock of—"

"Marlena." Alise cut her off. "Don't try to pretend you've never gotten taken in by a bad boy. What about Troy Hopkins in college?"

The smug lawyer blushed. "I was young. I didn't know better, and besides, it's hard to resist a guy who looks that good in a pair of jeans."

Alise giggled. "Apparently, half the girls on campus felt the same way. He had so many girlfriends Marlena had to book her dates three weeks in advance."

"Yeah, yeah, yeah. Enough about me," Marlena said, draining her glass.

"Well, everybody already knows my story." Alise rolled the edge of her cocktail napkin between two fingers. "I'm lucky I finally got rid of Ron before he spent what was left of my 401K. What about you, Rennie? Have you ever dated a *bad* boy?"

"No," she answered without thinking as she scanned the dance floor.

There hadn't been many men in her life. The few she'd dated in college were bookish introverts who'd had no problem keeping her company in the library on Saturday nights. Getting a scholarship to college had been an opportunity she'd had no intention of wasting.

Rennie had stayed out of the social scene, partially out of self-preservation and partially because she'd been too numb inside to allow herself any fun.

"You've never dated a bad boy? Not even in high school?" Alise asked. "No guys who drove too fast or smoked under the bleachers?"

"Uh...well, maybe one. But everyone just *thought* he was a bad boy. He really wasn't." Rennie stiffened. At least, she hadn't thought so at the time.

"I see. It's the old 'he's just misunderstood' routine," Marlena said. "Okay, I'll bite. Why did everyone *think* he was a bad boy?"

Rennie bit her lip. "Because he was in a gang." She felt her face heat, knowing how incriminating her words sounded. Alise and Marlena had grown up in normal suburban households. She couldn't expect them to understand how complicated circumstances had been then.

"Whoa." Alise's eyes went wide.

"A gang?" Marlena looked intrigued.

"As in Crips and Bloods? That type of a gang?"

Rennie shifted uncomfortably in the booth. "Sort of, but it was a much smaller local gang." Why had she opened her big mouth?

Marlena grinned wickedly, clearly enjoying herself. That meant she was getting ready to grill Rennie over an open flame. "So, Ren, how did *your* guy look in a pair of jeans?"

Rennie was surprised that she still felt a gnawing ache in her heart when she allowed herself to think about Gray. So many regrets. So many what ifs. But despite the sting, her body still remembered him with heat that could burn white-hot.

"He was really good-looking," Rennie said, wishing she hadn't allowed herself to become the center of attention. "He was light-skinned with a body like a Chippendale's dancer. Need I say more?" Her description didn't do him justice, but it was enough to satisfy her friends.

Alise pushed her daiquiri, half full, to the side so she could lean closer to Rennie. "What was he like?"

"He was sweet. Gray looked out for me. He made sure no one bothered me, and—"

"Gray?" Marlena's brow wrinkled. "Is that his real name?"

Rennie shrugged. "His first name is Keshon, but his mother named him after an uncle who was, as he liked to say, a few ants short of a picnic. Everybody's always called him Gray."

"So give us the dirt, girl." Marlena was through warming up. She was ready to get tough. "So far you're making him sound like a Boy Scout, but a guy who ran with a gang can't be a complete angel."

"I'm not saying he was, but it's not

what you think. The only reason he joined was to look out for my older brother.''

''Your brother was in a gang?'' Lines of confusion creased Alise's forehead. ''I didn't even know you had a brother. You never mention him.''

''He was killed when I was fourteen.'' Rennie drained the rest of her margarita without tasting a drop of it. Suddenly, she felt exposed. That was a time in her life she didn't want to revisit.

Her friends made sympathetic coos before falling into silence. Rennie banged on the table. ''Hey, what's with the long faces? I didn't mean to bring everybody down. We came out tonight to have fun.''

Alise still looked a bit stunned, but Marlena immediately picked up on Rennie's plea to change the subject. She signaled for the waitress.

''When is your girl Sarita performing, Ren? I'm in the mood to kick up my heels.'' Marlena wriggled her shoulders to the music.

Rennie looked at her watch. ''She should be taking the stage any minute now.'' Sure enough, a few minutes later, the lights dimmed and Sarita was introduced.

The curtain parted, revealing a bandstand in front of a giant sand castle. Red and yellow spotlights swirled, and Sarita ran on stage wearing a short dress in a stunning electric blue. The lights went up, and she began to sing a swinging salsa number. The infectious tempo of the conga drums had Rennie and her friends dancing in their seats. It wasn't long before Marlena stood, grabbed a guy lounging at the bar and began spinning around the dance floor.

Sarita sang four more songs before the lights dimmed on stage and she disappeared behind the curtain.

Marlena returned to the table, dabbing her forehead gently with a cocktail napkin. "That was fun. Why didn't you guys come out?"

Alise laughed. "We didn't feel like being upstaged. Where did you learn those fancy dance steps?"

"My ex-boyfriend taught me to salsa. He was a really boring date until you got him on the dance floor. Too bad he never learned to move his hips like that off the dance floor." The three women shared another round of raucous laughter.

Rennie nudged Alise so she could slide out of the booth. "I'm going to try to catch up with Sarita backstage. I'll be back in a few minutes."

Gray entered the storage room behind Ocean's Sand Castle Lounge, where Flex and Los were stacking crates. Despite the years they'd spent apart, Gray knew the guys working with him would take a bullet for him just as quickly now as they would have at sixteen when they'd been running the streets together.

There were five of them left, including Gray, and nothing bonded a group of men together more than knowing each one would die for the other. That's what being in a gang meant. It was family—bound together by choice rather than genetic obligation. It meant never being alone or on your own.

That simple truth should have made things easier for Gray, but a lot of the time it only made what he had to do more difficult.

"Hey, G." Los passed with a loaded hand truck, humming the theme song to "The Jeffersons."

"Hey. I tried to break away in time to help you guys unload the truck, but I got tied up working the door." Gray walked over to the closest shipment. "Kalashni-kovs?"

"Yep, sixty crates," Flex answered, stacking the last one.

Gray rubbed his hands together. "Let's have a look."

Los handed him a crowbar, and Gray brushed away the packing material to inspect the gun.

Flex leaned forward, issuing a low whistle. "Man, that is *tight*. When you gonna hook me up with one of those?"

Gray's laugh had an icy edge. "We don't deal on the front lines anymore. Don't think street thug, think businessman. Trust me, if you find yourself in need of this kind of hardware on the regular, you're doing something wrong."

"Yeah." Los smacked Flex in the back of the head.

Flex shrugged. "Hell, I just thought I

might, you know, start a collection or something.''

Gray opened a few more crates and did a quick count to make sure all the guns were accounted for. The client for this particular shipment wasn't one of the heavy hitters, but Gray had built a reputation for providing reliable service, and these small-time deals were starting to lead them to the big ones.

The biggest problem Gray had faced in the last few months was convincing his boys to look at the big picture. When he'd rolled into town, they were still committing petty crimes with quick payoffs they could blow through in less than a day. Most of them didn't have the patience for the kind of jobs that would bring in real money.

Their world hadn't changed much while he'd been gone. Success was still measured more by what you owned than by how you lived. In the neighborhood they had all grown up in, the trick had been to live hard and collect as many toys as possible because no one expected to live long.

Life had a different value on their side of town. A good pair of athletic shoes was worth more than a kid's life. For teenagers, even light conversation was heavy. Instead of talking about which couples were hooking up or breaking up, they talked about who'd been shot lately. Instead of fantasizing about the kinds of jobs they would get or the houses they would buy, they picked out the music for their funerals and the types of caskets they wanted.

How, Gray wondered, was anyone supposed to have hope for the future? For them, a better life just didn't exist.

This was it. The only way out of the ghetto was drugs and guns. So why not do it right? No more petty thieving. No more quick payoffs. Why not hold out for the big score? They knew how to get the money, but it took a lot of planning and patience.

The transition from street thug to businessman had been easiest for Los, who looked more like a fashion model than a common thug, anyway. He was willing to do anything that would bring in enough loot to keep him in designer clothes, trendy cars and materialistic women.

Franco, Los's younger brother, who was tending bar in the VIP lounge, wasn't much of a problem, either. He did whatever his older brother told him to do, but Woody and Flex were another matter.

Woody had gotten his leg shot off in a drive-by when he was eighteen. Even though his prosthesis wasn't really made of wood, no one could resist the nickname. He hadn't been too keen on the idea of checking ID and collecting cover charges at the door. He and Flex still didn't understand why they had to do real work at the club in addition to their private endeavors. But their positions at Ocean were crucial to the operation.

As long as they got their work done and made regular contributions, Ocean's manager, Paul Nocchio, didn't care what other business the men conducted on the side. It hadn't taken Gray long to make connections with local arms dealers and begin to funnel business through the club. With just a few deals, he'd been able to start swimming with the big fish.

Now he planned to catch himself a shark.

Sarita leaned over and gave Rennie a hug. "Thank you so much for coming, chica."

Rennie squeezed her in return. "Thanks

for the invitation. We're having a great time. Are you doing another set tonight?''

Sarita nodded. ''One more at ten-thirty. Then I'm going home to get some sleep. I was so keyed up about this performance that I didn't sleep at all last night.''

''Then I'll let you get ready,'' Rennie said, backing toward the door. ''I'll see you at our group session tomorrow evening?''

''You bet.'' Sarita walked her to the door. ''Do you know how to get out? This place can be confusing, and all the doors backstage look the same. Make sure you leave through the second door. Otherwise, you'll end up in the storage room.''

Rennie stepped into the hallway, feeling a rush of pride for Sarita. She'd come such a long way in just nine months. When Rennie met her, Sarita had been dancing in a run-down strip bar trying to pay for her sister's hospital bills after the younger

girl had her face slashed by an all-girl
gang. It had taken Rennie months to get
Sarita to trust her.

Now Sarita was going to nursing
school, working part-time at the hospital,
and she'd even met someone special. Her
new boyfriend, who worked as a bouncer
at Ocean, had helped Sarita get this singing gig. Rennie smiled. She was really beginning to feel like she'd made a difference in the young woman's life.

Rennie was so caught up in her
thoughts, she forgot Sarita's instructions.
Not sure which of the identical doors led
to the club, Rennie exited through the first
one she came to.

"Oops," she exclaimed as three men
immediately whirled around. "Sorry, I
think I'm lost—"

Somewhere in her subconscious, Rennie knew her mouth had stopped forming
words and her lower lip was hanging

lamely, but she was powerless to do anything about it.

Rennie had been hit by a wave of recognition so strong, it forced her backward several steps. Blinking rapidly, she tried to pull herself together, struggling to catch her breath. Had that one margarita given her hallucinations? It just couldn't be....

"Gray? Is that you?" she whispered.

Chapter 2

"Rennie..." In the split second it took for Gray to register her presence, several emotions jolted through him like bolts of lightning.

Some of the sensations he was feeling were reflected in her eyes, like the surprise and excitement, the regret...and especially the pain. The sight of her brought an immediate and stabbing ache ten times more intense than what he'd felt each time he'd thought of her over the years.

But one emotion was entirely his own,

and it took precedence over all the others. That emotion was raw, undiluted fear.

It kept him rooted to the spot, staring and shaking his head, until someone cleared a throat behind them, launching him into action. He pulled her to him in a brief embrace, and in one motion spun her around to face the door. Taking her elbow, he led her to the corridor. ''Now that you know what's behind door number one, let's try door number two.''

They were both silent as he guided her to the main room of the club. To avoid losing her in the crowd, he took her hand and pulled her toward a roped-off staircase. ''The VIP section of the club is upstairs. It's much less crowded there.''

Gray didn't just want to get her to a quiet corner where they could talk, he wanted to get her as far away from the gun shipment as possible. It made him crazy to think about how close she'd come to seeing something she shouldn't have back there.

He still didn't know how to process her sudden appearance. When he'd come back to L.A., he hadn't believed for a second that he might run into Rennie. When she left him to go to college in Texas, he'd been certain she wasn't coming back.

This was the last place he would have chosen for their reunion.

Gray led her to the bar, releasing her hand, which had been trembling in his. Clearly, she was as nervous at this unexpected meeting as he was. "Can I get you a drink?"

"Just water."

While he gave her order to Franco, in the mirror he saw her run a self-conscious hand over the back of her hair.

Rennie had nothing to worry about. She looked perfect. As a teenager, she'd been pretty, with lots of potential. As an adult, she was heart-stopping. Especially in that short, clingy little dress she was wearing.

After he handed her the glass, Gray motioned her to a quiet corner table. Once she was seated across from him, she gulped her water, as if to avoid being the first to speak.

He smiled at her, trying to put her at ease. "It's good to see you."

She nodded. "Yes, it is. I mean it's good for me to see you. That is, good to see you, too."

He couldn't help laughing out loud. "Yes, I knew what you meant."

"This is so strange. I was just talking about you to a couple of my girlfriends."

"Did you come with them tonight?" It hadn't occurred to him until that moment that she might have come with a date. His eyes darted to her left hand. No wedding band.

"Yes, I did. We're having a sort of... girls' night out...thing."

Gray felt a smile curling his lips again. He'd never seen her this frazzled before. He made another attempt to get her to lighten up. "Are you sure that water isn't going to your head? Maybe I should have the bartender cut you off for the night. Or maybe you need something stronger. Relax," he said, touching the back of her hand.

She pulled back as though he'd burned her, then tried to cover her reaction by grabbing her water glass and draining it as if it were a fifth of Scotch. "I know you must think I'm wound too tight, but I wasn't prepared to see you here. It's kind of spooky, really. Because, like I said, I was just talking about you. It's as if you walked right out of my thoughts."

"You were just talking about me, huh? What did you say?"

She shrugged and then began looking around as though she couldn't get enough of the blue velvet upholstery, marble floors or scenic ocean tapestries. Clearly she wanted to change the subject.

He opened his mouth to ask her if she'd moved to the city or was just visiting when she turned to him.

"So, how was prison? I mean, how have you been?"

Gray flinched before he could stop himself. He didn't know who had told her, and it really didn't matter. The bottom line was that...she *knew*.

"I'm sorry. That was a stupid thing to say. I don't know why I blurted that out like that."

He felt his whole body go cold, and he welcomed the numbness that came with it. Gray raised his gaze to hers. Neither her stunned expression nor the hint of a blush on her mahogany cheeks fazed him. Sure, she hadn't meant to be so blunt, but he knew exactly what she saw when she looked at him—an overgrown thug and an ex-convict.

The fact that he'd been to prison must have been on her mind the entire time. For all he knew, she'd been acting so rattled out of fear instead of nerves.

His mind replayed the image of her flinching when he'd touched her.

"Don't apologize. I know why you said it. You want me to tell you it isn't true, right?"

She seemed to be holding her breath. "*Is* it?"

"Sorry to disappoint you, sweetheart. It's true."

Rennie chewed on her lower lip. "What happened?"

He laughed. "Well, it was a weapons charge. You see, the police found two hundred Russian assault rifles in my possession, and they just wouldn't accept 'I'm a collector' for an explanation.'' He ended with a sarcastic chuckle.

''I don't think it's funny.''

''Really, you don't? Gee, that's odd, because I thought getting arrested was funny. And getting convicted—that was hilarious. And I thought I would die laughing when they sent me to—''

''That's enough. You don't have to make fun of me.''

Gray knew he was being cruel, but he couldn't stop himself. It surprised him how much resentment he felt toward her at that moment.

Of all the clubs in L.A., why did she have to pick this one? If she'd stayed in Texas, she might never have known if he were dead or alive, but that would still be better than returning to find her worst fears confirmed.

Gray could see her disappointment. Before she left she'd told him how much she believed in him. She was getting out of the inner city, and she'd been certain that he would, too. Instead, she found just the opposite. If she stuck around long enough, she'd discover he'd given an old adage new meaning—if you can't beat 'em, take over.

"I guess a lot has happened since the last time we saw each other," she said.

Gray expelled a harsh laugh. "You can say that again."

Rennie stared at her hands. They were trembling slightly.

Instantly, he felt terrible for upsetting her. None of this was her fault. He couldn't say anything to change her mind about him. Lying to her was surprisingly easy, but it was killing him that he had to.

He forced himself to get a grip on his temper, taking a moment to study her. Her hair was short now. She'd traded in the ponytails and French braids he remembered for a slick, trendy cut that flattered her gamine features.

"You look beautiful...and successful," he said, noticing the diamond studs sparkling in her ears. He was glad she'd moved up in the world, but part of him still wished she hadn't had to leave him to do it. "What have you been doing with yourself?"

"I'm a psychologist."

"Perfect. I bet you have your own office where the rich and pampered of Beverly Hills make weekly appointments to whine about their overindulgent mothers and their cold, stern fathers." Despite his best effort, he couldn't keep the sarcasm out of his voice. Things were going from bad to worse.

Rennie's lips twisted at his mockery. "Well, you're right about one thing. *Only* one thing. I do have my own practice. But it's in downtown L.A., not Beverly Hills. I work at the Help Center. I counsel women who have been battered or abused.''

Gray opened his mouth to respond, but Rennie cut him off. ''So what about you? You're what? A bouncer here?'' Her tone was imperious.

''That's right. You know there aren't a whole lot of options for an ex-con.''

Rennie stood from the table. ''My friends are probably worried by now. I'd better get back to them. Uh, it was…nice seeing you again.''

''No, it wasn't.'' He stood, too. ''Not as nice as it should have been. But, like you said, a lot has happened since we last saw each other, Rainbow,'' he said, using his old nickname for her.

He could tell he'd caught her off guard. The change in her demeanor was immediate. The line of her lips softened, and her eyes became dewy.

In that split second, they were transported back to a time where only the two of them existed. Before she had a chance to recover, he leaned down and brushed his lips against hers. He needed to be close to her for just a moment. He had to have a memory to carry with him.

"You take care of yourself," he said, pulling back.

She nodded and bolted down the stairs and, most likely, out of his life.

After Rennie left, Gray stayed behind trying to make some sense out of what had just happened.

Franco walked over and sat down across from him. "Hey, G, what's up with TK? You cutting him in?"

Gray looked up slowly. He hadn't been

expecting to hear that name for a while. "What do you mean? He's in prison."

"Not any more." Franco grinned. "Los says a key witness just...disappeared." He snapped his fingers to demonstrate. "They had to let him out."

Gray felt his lips tighten. Once upon a time, TK had been their gang leader. "Where have you seen him?"

Franco shrugged. "He's come around a few times. I thought he would have caught up to you by now."

"Is he looking for me?" It was clear that TK had been avoiding him. That could only mean trouble.

Franco sobered, finally realizing that Gray wasn't as thrilled with the news as he'd expected. "I don't know, but he knows we're all working here with you. So, you gonna cut him a piece of the action, or not?"

''We'll see. If you run into him again, tell him I want to talk to him.''

Franco nodded. ''I'm going on my break. Later.''

After Franco left, Gray swore under his breath. It wasn't hard to imagine what was going through TK's mind right now. He'd always had grandiose dreams about the money and power they were all going to have, but he'd never been able to make it happen. He was sloppy and he'd kept getting caught. Once TK had started going in and out of prison, the gang had fallen apart. Now it seemed Gray had stepped into his shoes and taken over his dreams—and he was succeeding.

Gray knew TK wouldn't appreciate having to be cut in on his old territory. When Gray came back to L.A., he'd heard TK was up on murder charges, tied up in a trial that should have dragged on for months. Gray hadn't expected to have to deal with TK at all.

Back in the day, Gray and TK had never agreed on anything. If TK did want a piece of their operation, it wouldn't be long before he tried to run things again. Gray couldn't let that happen. There were too many other forces at work here.

Still, he couldn't quite leave TK out in the cold. His men wouldn't understand. It didn't even matter that their old gang no longer existed in its original form. They would always be bound together by the old codes and traditions.

Dealing with TK was going to be tricky. Now that he was out of prison, he'd expect things to go back to the way they were when they were all banging. It would be useless to try to convince him that those days were over.

After all, everyone knew that the only way out of a gang was to die out.

Chapter 3

Gray awoke the next morning to the persistent ringing of his doorbell. Cursing as he dragged on his jeans, he hopped to the door and shouted, ''Who is it?''

''Overnight Express.''

Gray rolled his eyes and jerked the door open.

On the surface, nothing seemed out of the ordinary about the dark-haired package carrier dressed in the standard polo-shirt-and-shorts uniform. The man narrowed his green eyes, squinting at the envelope in his hand. ''I've got a delivery here for Kee...Keesh—''

Gray snatched the envelope out of his hands. ''Shut up and get in here.'' Glaring at his partner and longtime friend Seth Greene, he tugged on the thread unsealing the letter. ''I don't suppose you could have waited until a decent hour?''

Seth made himself at home on Gray's sofa, propping his feet on the coffee table. ''Ten o'clock *is* a decent hour for most people.''

''Maybe, but you know I had to work at the club until three last night.''

''Anything interesting happen?'' Seth rested a throw pillow behind his head.

Gray dropped the envelope without looking at the contents, shoving Seth's feet down from the coffee table. Oh, yeah, something very interesting happened. Unfortunately, it had nothing to do with his assignment.

There was no point in telling Seth about Rennie, though she'd been on his mind constantly since he'd laid eyes on her last night. It didn't matter, because he wouldn't be seeing her again.

"Actually, there is something that you should probably check into. TK, the guy who ran the gang I used to hang with, has turned up. I haven't seen him myself, but it's only a matter of time."

"What's his story?" Seth propped his feet back on the table. "He heard you were back in town and wants in on the action?"

Gray shook his head. "I'm not sure yet what he wants. But it's a safe bet that he's not going to like the fact that I'm sort of in control now."

"So you think he's going to make trouble? Maybe even try to take over," Seth concluded.

"No doubt." Gray propped himself on the arm of the sofa.

"I'll see what I can get on him."

"That shouldn't be too difficult. He was just up on murder charges. I don't know the details, but the witness has apparently disappeared. It's a safe bet that you'll find TK behind it."

"Got it. In the meantime—" Seth picked up the envelope he'd brought Gray "—here's the list of names you need. These are all the major players. Seems things are going well. Your name is spinning in all the right circles. The word on the street is that you're the man to see if you want to get into the drugs and weapons game in L.A."

"Gee, wouldn't Mom be proud."

Seth scowled at him. "What's gotten into you?"

"Nothing." Gray took the paperwork and shoved Seth's feet off the table one final time. "I'll look over these names just as soon as you leave."

Seth stood and Gray followed him to the door. "Who are you kidding, Gray? You're not getting ready to get to work on anything but a mattress and a pillow."

Gray clapped Seth on the back, partially as a friendly gesture of farewell and partially to urge him to the door faster. "Where in the secret spy handbook does it say that a good agent is sleep deprived?"

Seth grinned. "Right under the paragraph where it says all uniforms worn in the line of duty will be itchy and at least one size too small." He tugged irritably at his collar.

After Seth left, Gray considered going back to sleep, but he was entirely too restless to relax. He went into his bedroom and spread the contents of the envelope across his desk. There were pictures and bios of all the major drug lords in L.A. Several of them, Gray had already had dealings with.

Eventually, the connections Gray was making would lead him to SPEAR's nemesis. They'd been tracking him for some time and were making slow but steady progress. They knew the traitor was going by the name Simon. Other agents had connected him to both the Brotherhood of Blood, a hate group in Idaho, and to terrorists in the Middle East. Most recently, a SPEAR operative encountered Simon in the flesh, giving them a face to go with the name.

Gray's mission wasn't simple, but he hoped to dispose of Simon once and for all. He couldn't let Jonah down.

Jonah was the head of SPEAR and had been for as long as anyone could remember. Only no one had ever gotten the chance to look Jonah in the eye. To most

SPEAR agents, he was a voice and a reputation.

But when he gave orders, no one dared question them.

Now that Gray had made a name for himself in the L.A. drug trade, it wouldn't be long before Simon came to him.

Gray pulled out his laptop and connected it to a secured cable modem. He logged onto the SPEAR ISP, intending to send e-mail inquiries regarding his new contact list. Instead he found himself typing the name Rennie Williams into an encrypted search engine. In all the years he'd been an agent, he'd always managed to resist the urge to check into Rennie's whereabouts. He'd squashed that compulsion by reminding himself that he was better off not knowing any details.

But now that he'd seen her face to face and looked into those soft brown eyes, he had to know the full story. She was a psychologist. That didn't surprise him. She'd always had a huge heart and a deep concern for others.

In less than ten seconds, Gray had a full-page printout on Rennie. He stared at the sheet of paper, then crumpled it up and threw it in the wastebasket.

What was he doing? He couldn't see her again. Especially not now. In her mind he was a criminal. A former gang member who had lived up to all of society's expectations for him. He'd moved from a life of street violence to the ever-popular country club of crime, the state penitentiary.

She had no idea that her leaving him was probably the only thing that saved him from that inevitable reality. Rennie couldn't know that she'd inspired him to escape, as well, to flee their destitute neighborhood of hopelessness and poverty just the way she had.

When Rennie left for school, he'd been bitter. Hadn't she trusted him? Hadn't she believed him when he'd promised to find a way out for both of them? Gray had asked himself those questions time and again. But the feelings of hurt and anger hadn't lasted. Once they'd faded, Gray had been left with an almost desperate desire to prove that he could get out, too.

Soon after Rennie left, Gray's mother had been taken by the cancer that had been eating away at her life and spirit for almost a decade. He had no more ties in the neighborhood. He no longer had an excuse for staying with the gang. After a couple of months of aimless wandering, he joined the United States Marines.

That move changed his life forever. He'd shown a natural talent for most things he'd tried. And it wasn't long before his intelligence and skills had gotten him noticed by an exclusive, invisible

government agency, SPEAR. He passed
their rigorous testing process and was re-
cruited.

He was a secret agent with boyhood images of fighting terrorists and busting up
political conspiracies. Only Gray's first assignment had sent him right back to the
streets of south central L.A.

He jumped right into the middle of an
illegal arms dealing operation, got the au-
thorities all the information they needed
and then was publicly arrested right along
with the others. He spent two weeks in jail
to solidify his cover and then was shipped
off to his next assignment.

But those two weeks in jail changed
him like no other life experience could.
The world he became privy to in that short
time made him all the more determined to
keep fighting what seemed to be a never-
ending war against crime. It chilled him
to his soul, because if it weren't for the

grace of God, he might have filled those shoes in reality. The fact that he was inside for the good guys made that truth all the more poignant.

Growing up, he'd heard all the speeches from the ministers and do-gooders in the community. They especially loved the sound bite that black men in the inner city were an endangered species. In danger of succumbing to gangs, crime, violence, prison and ultimately death because society didn't have enough good role models for the urban black male.

That line never meant much to Gray until he went to prison, but then he got a close look at what society had discarded. Men who'd never had any hope or belief that they could be anything more than what they were. And in just two weeks' time, even though he was in jail under pretense, he began to get sucked into that world of hopelessness. He'd felt the black

hand of despair reaching out to him. It had
had him by the collar and would have had
him by the throat if he hadn't been transferred so quickly.

Even though his next assignment had
him drinking champagne at political dinners as an African diplomat trying to
smooth over a potential international incident, he never forgot what it felt like to
be in prison. It was a lesson he used daily
to remind himself that there was no room
in his life for screwups.

When Rennie left L.A. nine years ago,
the chances of her returning permanently
had been slim at best. But after receiving
her Ph.D. in psychology, Rennie surprised
herself by turning down a teaching position at the University of Texas for an opportunity to set up her own practice. And
it just happened to be six blocks from her
old neighborhood.

The Los Angeles Help Center was a three-story apartment building that had been turned over to the community. Inside were offices offering a variety of social services, including family planning, addiction and crisis counseling and Rennie's women's counseling practice. The Help Center attracted some difficult clients, but during the past year, she'd found the work truly rewarding.

Rennie sank further into her wing chair as Sarita and the other women in her counseling session argued. The clock on the far wall read twenty past four. She should have broken up this heated disagreement a long time ago, but she'd been a bit distracted today.

"I don't care what you say," Sarita said. "Farah is not breaking up with Will. She's just taking time to figure out what she wants."

Jackie crossed her heavy arms over her

substantial bosom. "Will is history. Get used to it. Now that Farah knows her daughter Lily is having Will's baby, there's no way she's going to take him back." Even under the best circumstances, Jackie didn't have a forgiving nature. This was probably the reason men feared her.

"Well, I think it's about time she got rid of that bum," Moni said. "Everyone can see that Brock is in love with Farah. Once he recovers from his liver transplant, he's going to tell her how he feels." Moni had always believed that love conquered all, which explained why she focused her energy on keeping a man instead of keeping a job.

"Good luck," Carla said, ever the pessimist. "I'll bet you an entire case of snack cakes that Brock is dead before the end of the week."

"Okay, okay." Rennie held up two fingers. "That's enough commentary on 'To

Love and to Cherish.' Doesn't anyone have any real issues to discuss today?''

Rennie let her gaze rest on each of the four women in turn. Silence. ''What about you, Carla? What's on your mind?''

Instead of harping on her good-for-nothing husband, as expected, the petite blonde looked at the soda can in her hand. ''If you want to know the truth, I really wish you'd keep more diet soda in the refrigerator. This is the second week in a row that I've had to drink regular.''

Rennie resisted the urge to roll her eyes. ''Carla, I've told you before that you're free to bring whatever you want to keep in the fridge. I could go broke trying to cater to everyone's snacking preferences. That said, I think there's one more diet cola hidden in the vegetable crisper.''

Carla let out a joyful squeal and headed to the kitchenette.

"What about you, Jackie?" Rennie asked.

"Hey, yeah. Carla, bring me an orange, will ya?"

Rennie sighed. Normally she loved the apartment-style setup of her office. The comfortable sofas and overstuffed chairs usually helped her clients feel more relaxed. But there were times when the unconventional surroundings worked against her.

In the beginning, Rennie had met with each woman individually, trying to work through the worst of their problems. Once their lives began to turn around, she brought them together, hoping the women could benefit from a support system of their peers.

The group had been meeting twice a week for a little over a month, and it had been working quite well. Much of the time, Rennie could guide the discussion and then allow the other women to offer guidance and support to whoever was having a problem at the moment. As an added bonus, the women were becoming real friends. Most days, this was a good thing.

But, on days like today, it could be a problem. Combine their chatty mood with the cozy living room setup, and trying to get any genuine feedback this late on a Friday was nearly impossible. Under normal circumstances, Rennie knew just how to keep the women on track, but right now even she was having trouble focusing.

No matter where her thoughts traveled, they always came fluttering back to Gray. She wanted to kick herself every time she remembered the disastrous conversation she'd had with him—

Rennie's head jerked up as a pair of fingers snapped in front of her face. Sarita backed up and sank into her recliner.

"Welcome back, Rennie. Did you have a good trip?"

Heat suffused her cheeks as Rennie realized she'd been caught daydreaming. She tried to play it off. "So, have you all decided what you'd like to discuss today?"

Moni nodded. "Yeah, I'd like to know what's up with you. First of all, you never let us get away with chitchat for more than fifteen minutes. Today you let us talk for almost half an hour."

"Plus," Jackie added. "You've been staring off into space all day. What's on *your* mind?"

"It's got to be a man," Carla said. "When a woman has problems, it's *always* a man." She was the only married member of the group, and ironically the only one who didn't want to be.

Rennie shook her head. "This is not about me. We're supposed to be talking about the issues that the four of you are dealing with.''

Sarita grinned. ''Well, Miss Thang, thanks to you, all of us are doing just fine right now. Looks like you're the one with a lot of junk on your mind. Are you too good to let us psychoanalyze you for a change?''

''Yeah.'' Carla cheered, taking a long swig of her diet soda.

Rennie's first instinct was to protest. It wasn't her place to take up group time with her personal problems. But, as she looked at the expectant faces of the woman surrounding her, she began to think twice.

After some rocky months, they had all learned to open up to her and to each other. This was an environment of safety and trust that they'd created together. If Rennie chose to back off now, they might very well come to the conclusion that their trust had been misplaced.

"Okay, you win. It's not a big deal, but I do have something on my mind that I have mixed feelings about."

"Lay it on us, Rennie. We're all getting pretty good at this psychology stuff," Jackie said, sharing one section of her orange with Moni.

"All right. I ran into an old flame yesterday."

"Where?" Sarita asked. "At the club last night?"

Rennie nodded. "He caught me off guard, because I hadn't seen him since I moved to Texas to go to college several years ago."

"I see," Jackie said, putting on a dramatically serious face. "And what happened then?" The woman winked as if to say, "See, I can do this."

"We talked for a few minutes, but the

conversation went nowhere. To make a long story short, the last few years haven't gone as well for him as they have for me.''

''I see,'' Jackie said, tapping her chin with her index finger. ''How did seeing him again make you feel?''

''How did it make me feel?'' Rennie shook her head. There was no easy answer to that question. First, his soft, melting smile had thrilled her heart, then the hard shards of ice in his eyes had broken it. ''Strange. I said all the wrong things, and he's been on my mind ever since.''

''Has he been on your mind because you didn't like what you said to him or because you still feel some attraction to him?''

Rennie adjusted the collar of her shirt. Suddenly, it felt a bit constricting. ''Both.''

''So what do you think is going to make

you feel better about this situation?'' Jackie asked, turning Rennie's favorite phrase around on her.

''Well, for one thing, I want to apologize to him for the way our last meeting went. He's had some tough times, and I'm sure he thought I was judging him. We'd been close once, and I'd like the chance to be more supportive.''

''And the chance to see if there are any sparks left?'' Moni asked with a hopeful grin.

''I don't know. He may not be available anymore. There's been so much time between us, and we've both changed so much. I'm not even sure we still have anything in common.''

''So, what I hear you saying is that you want to see him again, but you're not sure if he's still single. If he is, are you interested?''

Rennie squirmed in her seat. They were

digging a little deeper than she was ready to go right now.

"Ha," Carla shouted. "It's not so easy in the hot seat, is it?"

Rennie laughed. "I must say, you guys are pretty good at this. I guess I should be flattered that you all were actually paying attention in our sessions."

Jackie looked at the clock. "We're almost out of time, but that doesn't mean you can wiggle out of the question. If your guy is available, would you be interested?"

Rennie shrugged. "I can't answer that right now."

"Okay, then what are your next steps?" Jackie had really gotten into her role. The words seemed to fall naturally from her lips.

"Find him and apologize, then I'll see exactly what's what."

"Perfect," Sarita said. "We'll follow up next week."

"No, next week I want to hear from every one of you. I let you off the hook this time, but next session we're getting back to business."

That afternoon, Gray got into his car and started driving. Before he realized where he was going, he found himself in front of the old building where Rennie worked.

Should he go inside? Her counseling sessions were for women only. No doubt he'd look conspicuous if he walked in. On the other hand, he probably didn't look any less conspicuous hovering around outside.

Before Gray could make a decision one way or the other, the matter was taken out of his hands. Rennie walked out of the front door. When she saw him standing there, she paused on the steps as if she'd seen a ghost.

Then she was moving again, her pace faster as she strode purposefully toward him. ''Hi.'' Her voice was breathy when she finally stopped before him.

''Hi, Rennie. Before you ask me what I'm doing here, let me start off by telling you right up front that I don't know. I got in my car and the next thing I knew I was here.''

She nodded, staring at her feet before finally lifting her gaze to meet his. ''This is so strange. Lately, it seems all I have to do is think about you, and you appear.''

He released the breath he hadn't known he'd been holding. Gray didn't know what he'd been expecting, but their reunion last night had seemed...well, bittersweet. In the bright light of day, or rather the dimming light of evening, she could have easily turned him away.

This was the last place he should be. Looking up an old flame had nothing to do with the job he'd come back to do. In fact, it could only get in the way.

"You've been on my mind, too. I didn't like the way we left things."

She bit her lip. "Um, is there somewhere we can go to talk? To catch up? I think I gave you the wrong impression last night...about your past. I'm not judging you—"

"Where do you want to go?" What was he doing? It wasn't too late to walk away.

But he stayed rooted to the spot, watching her face. He could stare at her face for hours. Periodically over the years, he'd wondered what kind of woman she'd become, and his imagination hadn't done her justice.

Her cheekbones, which had been round and full in youth, now arched high with the grace and beauty of maturity. Her skin was still as clear and perfect as it had always been, showcasing her pretty brown eyes and full berry-colored lips. Watching those lips, Gray couldn't help thinking about kissing them.

Rennie shifted her weight from foot to foot as if she were waging an internal debate. She still had the telltale habit of tapping her fingers on her thigh when she was conflicted.

"Rennie, we can do this another time," Gray said, trying to give her an out. It probably wasn't a good idea, anyway.

His voice seemed to bring her to a decision. "No, um, I really want to talk. Otherwise, I'll keep thinking about you—" She stopped abruptly and shook her head. "Not that there's anything wrong with thinking about you. That's not what I meant..."

Gray laughed. "I know what you meant." Last night, he'd mistaken her fluster for fear. It was a relief to know that she didn't think he was some kind of monster.

"Would you like to come back to my apartment? This isn't a come-on or anything. It's just that restaurants are noisy, and there isn't a lot of privacy with the waiters coming back and forth. My refrigerator isn't exactly fully stocked, but I'm sure we could scrape something up. I just don't want you to think—"

He reached out to touch the hand rapidly drumming on her leg, to halt both her fidgeting and her anxious ramble. "I'm not going to get any ideas. I promise. We'll just talk, okay?"

She nodded, clearly relieved. "Do you want to follow me? My apartment isn't far."

As Gray followed Rennie's lime green 1999 Volkswagen Beetle, he tried not to dwell on this reckless decision. He needed to see her. Once they talked about old times over a bite to eat, he'd go back to work at the club and put Rennie in a neat little package labeled *the past.* Maybe he'd be able to reopen that package one day, but for now, this one evening was all he could allow himself.

Twenty minutes later they pulled into a sophisticated apartment complex. She may work six blocks from the old neighborhood, but Rennie Williams had chosen to live in the suburbs. He couldn't fault her for that.

She parked her car and waited for him in front of the building.

"How long have you been living here?" he asked as they rode up on the elevator.

"A year next month."

"What made you come back? I thought when you left for Texas, you would end up settling down there."

Rennie sighed, as though thinking carefully about his question. "Well, after I got my Ph.D., I was teaching undergrad classes. One of my colleagues knew I had an interest in women's issues, so he told me there was a slot opening up at the L.A. Help Center. A literacy group had just relocated, and the Help Center board wanted to start a program targeted specifically to women," she said, unlocking her apartment door. "This is it." Rennie stepped back so he could precede her inside.

"This is a nice place. It's definitely you."

Though the room didn't look anything like Rennie's old bedroom, being inside her apartment gave him the same feeling. There weren't any beefcake posters or stuffed animals, but he could see hints of his old Rennie in this more mature and stylish room.

She still loved flowers. Instead of dotting her wallpaper, they were displayed in silk arrangements throughout the apartment. And she hadn't lost her appreciation for LL Cool J. Instead of hanging on her closet doors, he dominated the CD collection in the rack beside the stereo.

And there were new sides of her Gray hadn't experienced. Like the fact that she liked Japanese artwork. The room had elaborately painted silk screens and ornate fans hanging on the walls.

He moved to the bookshelf. "When did you start reading romance novels?"

"I use them at the Center to show battered women what a healthy relationship can be like. Since then, I've become a fan myself."

Gray continued to move around the room, asking Rennie about the knick-knacks or gadgets he came across. Each item was like a puzzle piece, completing his picture of the woman Rennie had become.

Finally he picked up a tiny frame, featuring an abstract collage of music notes with a French quote in the center. "Every soul is a melody which needs renewing," he read aloud.

Rennie turned. "Is that what it says? My friend Alise gave that to me because she liked the design. Since we'd both taken Spanish in high school, neither one of us could read the quote."

Gray realized immediately that he'd made a mistake.

"When did you learn to speak French?"

He couldn't tell her that since he'd joined SPEAR he'd become fluent in five languages, including French. Normally, sticking to his cover wasn't a problem, but because Rennie was tied to his past, things were complicated.

"No, I don't speak French. I've seen that frame before. The translation was written on a sticker on the back. I guess I just have a really good memory."

She studied him for a long moment. "I see. Well, make yourself comfortable while I see what kind of leftovers I have in the kitchen."

A few minutes later, Rennie entered the room. "I hope you aren't too hungry because all I have in the fridge are a pitiful collection of leftovers."

"I'm starving." Gray rubbed his grumbling stomach.

Rennie bit her lip. "We can order pizza."

"Let me take a look," he said, following her into the kitchen. "Remember, we used to come up with all sorts of masterpieces in your dad's kitchen."

"Oh, yeah." Rennie laughed out loud. "It's all coming back to me, and, as I re-

call, they were anything but masterpieces.''

After opening a few cabinets and carefully inspecting the refrigerator, Gray nodded to Rennie with confidence. ''Looks
like we have enough scraps here for a delicious Everything Stew.''

Rennie nodded. ''That doesn't sound
like a bad idea. Just point me in the right
direction.''

Gray was very at home in the kitchen.
Rennie showed him where things were,
and he was off and running.

Fifteen minutes later, Gray inhaled the
zesty vapor rising off their Everything
Stew. Pleased, he glanced at Rennie chopping carrots. ''This is going to be a good
one.''

She peeked over the edge of the pot.
''It's getting there,'' she said, dropping a
handful of carrot chunks into the mixture.

He stirred the pot, watching the colors

swirl together until a jumble of vivid memories began to bubble out of the stew along with the steam. "Remember the tomato and mayonnaise sandwiches we used to make?"

"Ugh." Rennie crinkled her nose. "That sounds so gross now. I can't believe we used to eat those."

"We ate 'em and loved 'em. They weren't so bad. Not much different than a BLT...without the B and the L."

Rennie laughed, placing a lid on the pot so the stew could simmer. "That's true. I guess tomato sandwiches weren't the worst concoctions we came up with."

Gray leaned against the counter, admiring the pristine condition of her kitchen. Clearly, she didn't like cooking any more now than she had when she was sixteen. The only well-used item in the room was her microwave.

"I think our worst culinary experiment

was our homemade macaroni and cheese.''

''I get sick just thinking about it,'' Rennie said, clutching her stomach. ''You know, I don't think I've eaten macaroni and cheese since that day.''

''That makes two of us. The macaroni and cheese disaster also put an end to our little kitchen experiments. After that we confined our after-school snacks to grilled cheese sandwiches or cereal.''

''I think *you* are responsible for my fear of cooking,'' she said, removing the lid on the pot to stir their stew. ''Thanks to you, I must exist on all things microwavable.''

''Don't blame me for that. In fact, you should be thanking me. Neither of us had a microwave back then. If it weren't for me, you wouldn't know how to work *any* kitchen appliances.''

The nights Gray had kept her company after school, it had been at his insistence that they attempt to make dinner for themselves. Otherwise, he was certain Rennie would have wasted away on pretzels and Froot Loops.

When the stew was ready, they set everything on the coffee table. Settling down on the floor before the table, Rennie sampled the first bite. "This isn't bad. Not bad at all."

Gray nodded his agreement after tasting his stew. The air in the kitchen had been filled with spiced cooking and memories, leaving no room for the tension that had been present since they'd seen each other again. But now that they had moved into the living room to eat their dinner, they fell into an awkward silence.

The tension drifted back, building a wall between them with bricks of uncertainty and fear. Gray watched Rennie's profile as she blew on her spoon before

sipping gently from it. How could someone so familiar be a complete stranger?

He paused, staring into his bowl as he
realized that statement could just as easily
be applied to him. He was nothing like the
Gray she once knew. It was obvious what
she saw when she looked at him. She must
have so many questions. Questions he had
no easy or truthful answers for.

Gray looked up to find that Rennie had
put down her spoon and was watching him
intently. "What's the matter?"

"I was just about to ask you the same
thing. Why the brooding look? Is something wrong with your stew?"

"No, my stew is fine."

"Then what's on your mind?"

"I was just thinking how, in some
ways, being here with you feels perfectly
natural. Like the years in between never
existed. But, in other ways, I look at you

and I can't help wondering about the hundreds of tiny things that I've missed.''

She looked at her bowl. ''I feel the same way.''

''There's something I want to ask you?''

''What is it?''

He reached out and touched her chin with his index finger. His thumb brushed over her lips. ''Why didn't you say good-bye before you left me?''

Chapter 4

Suddenly nine years of guilt came rushing back to Rennie. When she'd left for the University of Texas, it had been early morning. She hadn't awakened Gray to say goodbye. He deserved an explanation for that, but when she opened her mouth to speak, no words came out.

Stalling for time, she picked up their empty stew bowls and carried them into the kitchen.

Gray followed her. "We'd made plans, Rennie. We were supposed to wake up early together, then I was going to make you breakfast and take you to the airport. Instead, when I woke up, you were already gone.''

Rennie turned to face him, seeing raw emotion. It was as though she'd left him only minutes ago instead of years. Despite his words, she knew he wasn't asking, ''Why did you leave me that morning?'' He wanted to know why she'd left him at all.

She could only handle one thing at a time. The answer to the first question was easy.

''The night before I left, things had been so emotional and...intense. I'm not sure I would have been able to go if we'd gone through another scene like that.'' Rennie had nearly changed her mind about leaving California a thousand times. ''Getting on that plane was one of the hardest things I've ever done.''

He locked eyes with her, and she backed up into the dishwasher. "Then why did you? I told you that I would take care of you. Didn't you believe me?"

Finally, the question she'd been dreading. Rennie skirted around him and headed into the living room. Curling up on the couch, her bare feet tucked beneath her, she took a deep breath.

Gray sat on the floor, looking at her patiently. That was the problem with him. He'd always had an infinite amount of patience.

"This is one of the things I wanted to talk to you about. The best that I can do is try to explain what was going on in my mind at the time."

He nodded. "I'm listening."

"I'd lost my mom when I was only a baby and my father was *always* working, so my brother had been my whole world. I was only fourteen when Jacob died. You immediately stepped in to look out for me—walking me home from school, driving me to the grocery store, helping me with my homework. Whenever I needed you, you were there. And I began to count on that.''

''Are you trying to say that I—''

''Let me finish, Gray. It wasn't just me. When Jacob needed someone to watch his back, even though you'd turned down those thugs countless times, you joined the gang for his sake.''

''Not that it made any difference,'' he muttered, leaning against the couch so she could only see the back of his head.

''When I needed someone to play big brother, you were right there,'' she continued. ''And when I decided that I was tired of being a tomboy, you asked your mother to make me the most beautiful dress for the homecoming dance. And when my date got out of hand, you were there then, too.''

Rennie smiled, remembering what it felt like to have her own knight in shining armor that night. It had bolstered her feminine confidence to know that there was more than just brotherly overprotectiveness at work on Gray's part. He'd been jealous, and he'd proven it by taking her on their first date the next night.

''I'd had a crush on you for a while, but I think I fell in love with you that night.''

Gray looked at her in surprise. ''Really?''

She nodded. ''Yes. We were already close, but we became so much closer after that—and not just because we'd started dating. We shared our dreams and hopes for the future. I really got to know you as a person.''

''That's my point, Rennie, we shared

dreams. Then out of the blue you tell me you're applying to out-of-state schools. As proud as I was of you for getting accepted, I kept hoping you'd change your mind.''

''I wasn't *planning* to go to school so far away. But then Ronald Sharp was shot, and Gerald Nicks went to prison for it. Nisa Parker, who was supposed to be valedictorian, got pregnant and dropped out of school right before graduation. I started feeling the walls closing in on me. I wanted to see something outside of L.A. I could see how trapped you were—living your life for other people.''

''What the hell are you talking about?''

''You got mixed up in a gang trying to save my brother from himself. Then you couldn't get out of the gang because you were afraid they'd take it out on me. You couldn't go to any of the colleges you were accepted to because your mother was diagnosed with cancer, so you stayed to take care of her.''

He shrugged, shaking his head. ''What's your point?''

Rennie leaned down, forcing him to make eye contact. ''Can you name one life-changing decision you made back then that was just for *your* benefit and not someone else's?''

Gray was quiet for a long time, a grim expression on his face. ''I did what I had to do.''

''Yes, but I didn't want to be one more weight around your neck. I started thinking that if I stayed in L.A. you might never stop trying to take care of me. You wouldn't be free to make some choices of your own. And I had to start relying on myself. I couldn't keep waiting for you to save me.''

''So you decided to leave town.'' He shook his head. ''We made love for the first time the night before you left. Was that your way of saying goodbye to me?''

''Our first time wouldn't have had to be goodbye. I wasn't the one holding out on you. Don't you remember my seventeenth birthday?''

''Yes, I remember.'' A smile curved his lips, and he chuckled softly. ''You'd gone out for a movie and pizza with your girl-friends. Afterward, you showed up at my house. You told me that you wanted me to be your first.''

A hot blush stung her cheeks. ''That's right. And what did you say?''

He rubbed a hand over his forehead. ''I told you no,'' he said sheepishly.

''Exactly. And that wasn't the only time I'd offered myself to you, but you kept turning me down.''

''I wasn't rejecting you, Rennie. You know how badly I wanted you, but you were too young. You had your whole life ahead of you. I didn't want you to get pregnant and be tied down for the rest of your life.''

''We would have used protection.''

''I just didn't want you to become distracted from your goals. But apparently that wasn't a problem for you.''

Rennie chose to ignore his last remark. ''I finally seduced you our last night together. Why did you let me?''

He thought for a moment. ''I couldn't let you go away without physically showing you how much I loved you. And I just couldn't resist the look in your eyes. You looked like you needed me.''

Rennie caught her breath. ''I did need you.''

Gray reached up and put his hand on one of her bare feet. She shivered. Slowly he began to stroke the sensitive skin on the bottom of her foot.

She wriggled. ''That tickles.''

"You used to love to be tickled."

Rennie's face heated when she remembered all the times they'd sat in front of the television on her living room floor as kids. A tickling match would instantly become charged with sexual tension. Tension that would always go unrelieved, thanks to Gray.

He released her foot and pulled himself onto the sofa beside her. Their bodies didn't touch, but she could feel every particle of air that separated them.

He reached out and stroked his thumb over her chin. "Looking at you now, I can't for the life of me figure out how I managed to resist you for so long."

Rennie swallowed hard, cursing her body for its quick surrender. He'd only touched her chin, and already a deep, burning heat was stirring at her core.

Her lips parted, and she moistened them with her tongue. Gray's eyes locked on her mouth and she watched his nostrils flare slightly. Rennie sighed, feeling a surge of feminine power she hadn't felt in years.

Her eyes skimmed over him. Whatever the circumstances, the years had been good to his body. He'd always had a strong frame, but now the muscles outlining it were firmer and more defined.

Rennie's need for him was forceful and immediate. And there was curiosity.

Gray had been a sensitive and generous lover even as a young man. What would he be like in bed now? More aggressive, less sensitive? Or hotter and more deliberate? She wanted to know, intimately, what it would feel like to connect their past and their present.

For their first and only night together, she'd set the mood carefully. Before Gray had arrived, she'd set out the candles her father had kept in the kitchen drawer for emergencies. She put on a cassette of slow songs she'd spent the day recording from the radio and dressed in her best dress—a buttercup yellow summer dress Gray's mother had made before the cancer had forced her to stop working as a seamstress.

When Gray came to her door that night, she'd leaned up and poured her heart and soul into the kiss she gave him.

Wondering if his lips still had the same warm sweetness she hadn't experienced since, Rennie leaned forward. Guided by curiosity and the temptation of old memories, she went up on her knees, bringing her body flush with his. Then, cupping his chin, she leaned down and kissed him.

Gray's arms immediately folded around her back, bringing her down until she was cradled in his lap. The kiss had begun with the soft whisper of a memory but was flooded with the hot urgency of the moment.

Somewhere at the back of Rennie's mind, her emotions swirled out of control. Part of her was shocked that she was in Gray's arms. A place she never thought she'd be again. Another part of her, the most honest part, felt at home.

Her heart was an intricate puzzle, and an essential piece had been missing for years. Now that missing piece locked into place.

Gray's hands raked over her back. "Why can't I get enough of you?" he whispered against her chin. Then his hands found the edge of her shirt and slid beneath it. A violent shiver surged through her as his rough hands caressed the smooth skin of her back.

She mimicked his moves, letting her fingers run the length of the long, hard muscles of his back. Their mouths stayed connected as they pressed together, trying to merge their bodies into one. There was no time for extended foreplay. They both wanted the same thing.

''Where's your bedroom?'' Gray's voice was raspy.

''At the end of the hall.'' As soon as Rennie got the words out, Gray scooped her up and carried her down the hallway.

Inside the bedroom, Rennie sat on the edge of the bed, suddenly feeling nervous. Maybe they were letting their passions sweep them in to something they couldn't control? Before Rennie could consider this further, Gray pushed gently on her shoulders, and she went down on her back.

Kneeling over her, he removed her top and bra. Not wanting to be the only one topless, Rennie grabbed the bottom of Gray's T-shirt and began jerking it upward. She got as far as his shoulders and then Gray took over, stripping the shirt off in a single motion.

Rennie resisted the urge to moan at the

sight of his tightly muscled chest. She let her fingers play over the smooth ripples, frowning slightly as they found the smooth ridges of scars. One was an obvious bullet wound.

Before Rennie could dwell on it, Gray dipped his head and let his mouth devour her breast. He started with the nipple, which he flicked teasingly with the tip of his tongue. Then he let his lips close over the sensitized bud and sucked gently. Clearly wanting to give the other breast equal attention, he used his left hand to stroke and caress it until she released an anxious murmur.

At some point, while her mind was clouded with pleasurable sensations, Gray removed her jeans and underwear. Her hands immediately when to his pants, and once she had them unfastened, he helped her tug them off.

Both naked, their bodies came together.

"Rennie," Gray whispered at her ear. "I've fantasized about this for so long."

"So have I," she whispered back. "I never thought we'd be able to have this again."

"I just want to look at you."

Rennie forced herself not to squirm under the intensity of his gaze. Her body warmed as his fingers traced the path of his eyes from her face to the indent of her neck, where he paused to place a tiny sweet kiss.

As his eyes moved down her shoulders to her breasts, he used his tongue to mark all her most sensitive places. His thumb traced the fleshy swirl of her belly button to follow the dark line to her treasures below.

She felt the rough pads of his fingers and palms slide over her thighs, and it was almost too much for her to stand. She wanted to touch him, too.

When she tried to move, he pushed her fingers aside. "Hold on, baby, I'm not done looking at you."

With Gray, during lovemaking, looking was a five-sense event. While his eyes traced every delicate curve, his fingers touched, his tongue tasted, his nostrils inhaled her feminine scent, and he listened to her satisfied moans. She savored each minute of sweet torture.

After making sure she was protected, Gray sank into her and began to move with a mindless urgency. Rennie threw her head back and shut her eyes tight as she felt the pleasure building inside her. Gray showered her face with kisses, holding her tightly as he found his release.

Afterward, they lay together talking softly about anything and nothing. As the night drew on, Gray untangled himself from Rennie and started to dress.

Wrapped in nothing but a sheet, Rennie

lay on the bed watching him. "Are you sure you can't stay the night?"

He looked as reluctant as she felt. "I told you, I have to work at the club tonight."

A wicked expression came over her face. "Can't you call in sick?"

Gray fastened his belt and knelt on the bed, leaning down to give her a quick kiss. "Sweetheart, I would if I could."

She frowned, hating herself for feeling so needy. He hadn't even left yet, and she already missed him. "When will I see you again?"

He kissed her more thoroughly this time. "Very soon."

Gray walked into the smoky main room of Ocean like a zombie. He was on the verge of screwing up everything.

He couldn't say that making love to Rennie had been a mistake, but it certainly hadn't been a smart move. After tonight, Rennie couldn't help but think they were starting over. As much as he might like to, that just wasn't in the cards this time around.

Gray was in such a daze, he turned around swinging when he felt a hand on his shoulder.

"Whoa. Down, boy. Did prison make you jumpy, homes? It can do that to you if you don't know how to handle yourself."

Gray shook his head when he saw who was standing before him. The *last* person he needed to see at that moment.

"TK. I could ask you the same question. Seems you've gotten pretty good at sneaking up from behind."

TK shrugged. "I called your name but you didn't hear me. Gotta stay alert, dog."

Gray sized up TK quickly. Prison life had done nothing to tarnish TK's playboy good looks. But he seemed to lack the cockiness and confidence that had once backed his bold talk. Gray was looking into the eyes of a man who had nothing left to lose. That made him dangerous.

He had to tread lightly. "I heard you were around."

"That's right." TK made a slow rotation. "Had to check out the new digs."

"Like what you see?"

"It's not bad." He held up a champagne bottle and chugged from it. "Not bad at all."

"I see you found the Dom Perignon."

"Yeah, the boys hooked me up for old times' sake, you know?" TK's laughter trailed off.

Gray had had enough small talk. He needed to know exactly what TK was after. "What can I do for you, man?"

"Let me know the deal. You and all my

boys going legit or is there a little some-thin' you want to let me in on?''

Gray shrugged. ''You looking for a job?''

He had to make it clear that he was run-ning things. If TK wanted to be cut in, he had to know the score.

TK's mouth tightened, and his shoul-ders squared. The message had been re-ceived, but it wasn't going over well.

''Nah, man. I'm aiming for bigger and better these days. I've got something of my own going down. When everything comes together, some of the boys might want to come work with me.''

''They can come and go as they please. I'm sure they'll go wherever the money is. If your deal doesn't come through, just let me know.''

Gray said the words because he didn't have any other choice, but he hoped TK meant what he said.

"So you are running a game up in here?"

Gray simply smiled, neither confirming or denying the statement. "The job pays well."

TK stiffened. "Yeah, well, you watch yourself, Gray."

"Excuse me?"

He laughed with false levity. "Just a word of advice from an old pro. Back in the day, you had trouble hanging when the heat was on. Just want to make sure you can handle yourself under fire."

Gray showed TK his teeth. "You know something I don't?"

It was TK's turn to shrug. "No, no. I'm just saying, you've gotta watch your back when the stakes are high. I've been there. If you get in over your head, just let a brother know."

"Well, thank you, but I doubt that will be necessary. Good looking out, though."

"Any time, brother man. Any time."

Gray nodded curtly.

TK tipped his drink to Gray and walked away.

Gray stared after TK, hoping that Seth had been able to make some progress. His mission would run a lot smoother if they could get TK behind bars as soon as possible.

Gray made his rounds through the club, letting TK fade from his mind for the moment. Once his mind was free again, it immediately returned to Rennie.

Even though it would have been difficult, he should have let things go after their meeting in the club. Now he'd gone and started something he couldn't finish. She couldn't be a part of his life right now. Who knew when he'd be free to have a life of his own again.

Suddenly her voice echoed in his head. *Can you name one life-changing decision you made back then that was just for your benefit and not someone else's?*

Gray shook his head. This was no time to evaluate the circumstances of his life. He had a duty to perform, and his feelings for Rennie were already threatening to get in the way. That wasn't going to help either one of them. He needed to concentrate on his job, not get caught up in memories.

Since he couldn't tell her the truth, he'd only continue to disappoint her. Rennie had gone on to make a difference with her life. She didn't need to get involved with a man who appeared to be little more than an ex-con. He'd let her down enough for one lifetime.

It would be less painful for them both if he just stayed away.

The irony of their circumstances wasn't lost on him. They'd made love only one time before she'd left him nine years ago. Tonight they'd made love again, and this time, he had to leave her.

Chapter 5

Rennie woke up Sunday morning after a fitful night's sleep. She didn't want to believe the night she and Gray had spent together had been a mistake, but she had no idea what he was thinking. It had been a full day since she'd heard from him.

Rennie had spent most of Saturday replaying each moment she'd spent with Gray since he'd come back into her life. As time had ticked on with no word from him, her worries and feelings of self-doubt had mounted.

It didn't help her state of mind that her dreams had been filled with memories of the two of them. In most of them, they had been kids again. It was as if all the years that had intervened in their relationship hadn't existed.

Sitting up in bed, she hugged her pillow to her chest. Her mind was still reeling from the events of the last few days.

Rennie hadn't planned on sleeping with Gray when she'd invited him to her apartment—quite the opposite, in fact. Even now, she felt there were things that remained unresolved between them.

The fact that her leaving him still bothered Gray nine years later was very telling. He'd been through a lot in recent years and had changed so much. Maybe he wouldn't have lost his way if she hadn't abandoned him.

Rennie got out of bed and dressed, trying not to dwell on the fact that he hadn't called. They would have plenty of time to straighten things out. After all, he was back in her life again, and if their night together had proven anything, it was that they were still very good together.

For a while, their differences had melted away, and she'd felt connected to him again. She knew he'd felt it, too. Neither one of them could turn their backs on something so strong.

In time, Gray would begin to talk about what he'd been through since they'd parted. She couldn't expect him to open up right away, especially not after the way she'd put him on the spot during their first meeting.

Of course he felt as though he'd let her down by spending time in prison. She knew something like that had to be a blow to his pride in light of the morals and values he'd grown up with.

No matter where he'd been led astray,

Rennie believed she could help him come to terms with it. He had to forgive himself and know that she didn't hold his past against him. She knew what kind of man he was. She felt it in her heart.

Rennie made herself a late breakfast, trying to temper the anxious feelings roiling inside her. She wondered when she'd see Gray again. She wanted to tell him all the things she'd been thinking about since she'd seen him last.

She tried not to be overcome with anticipation as the day wore on. Gray hadn't left his phone number or told her where he was staying, so she had no way to contact him. Ocean was her only connection to him, and she didn't even know when he would be there.

Rennie also knew that Gray didn't have her phone number, but he did know where she worked and where she lived. Maybe he would drop by and see her.

She was trying to watch an old movie on television when her phone rang. Her heart began to thud rapidly in her chest.

"Hello," she answered.

"Hey, Ren. It's Alise."

She tried to keep her disappointment out of her voice. "Hey, girl, what are you up to?"

"I spent the whole day at the mall. I'm trying to get a head start on my Christmas shopping. Since I'm only ten minutes from your house, I thought I'd call and see if you want to have dinner."

Rennie was tempted to turn down Alise's offer, just in case she might hear from Gray, but she wasn't going to torture herself that way. She had to get her mind onto something else. It wasn't as though he'd been neglecting her for weeks. A couple of days was no big deal. He'd probably just gotten busy.

"Sure, Alise. That sounds like fun."

The two women picked a time and a place, and Rennie hung up.

An hour later, Rennie and Alise were seated across from each other at a sushi bar in the mall. First, Alise had to show her all the purchases she'd made that day.

"I hope Marlena likes this," she said, folding up a red cashmere sweater. "I picked it because she needs softer things in her wardrobe. She needs some clothes that aren't made of tweed or don't have pinstripes."

"She'll love it," Rennie said absently. She stared at the clock behind Alise's head. Maybe she should go check her messages. It was almost seven o'clock.

"You can't look at what's in *this* bag, Rennie. It's your gift."

"Okay." Maybe he couldn't find her number in the phone book and decided to drop by. What would he do when he discovered she was out?

"It's a pink elephant. Hard to wrap but I couldn't resist the color."

"I hope he leaves a note—huh? What...oops!" Rennie's eyes focused on Alise as she realized she hadn't heard a word her friend had been saying.

Alise shoved her shopping bags under the table. "What's gotten into you? Something is definitely on your mind."

Rennie sighed. "I have something to tell you."

Alise leaned forward. "Spill it."

"Remember that night at the club when we were talking about bad boys?" Her friend nodded. "Well, you're not going to believe this, but I ran into mine that same night. He's a bouncer for Ocean."

"You're kidding me. This is incredible." She sat up straight. "What happened between you two? No wonder you came back and gave us that lame story about getting lost."

"Actually, I did get lost. That's how I ran into him. I went through the wrong door after leaving Sarita's dressing room. I ended up in a storage room and there he was."

"Talk about timing. That's so weird."

"I know. Anyway he took me up to the VIP lounge so we could talk somewhere quiet."

"And..." Alise was clearly anxious.

"We practically got into an argument. A lot has changed since we last saw each other, and we were both on edge." She chose not to mention that the tension didn't crank up until she blurted out that Gray had been in jail.

"Wow, is that why you're so out of it tonight? You're upset over how the conversation turned out?"

"Not exactly. Friday evening he showed up at my office and we went back to my apartment to talk. We sort of smoothed things over.''

Alise touched Rennie's hand. ''That sounds like great news.''

''After the initial awkwardness, it really was nice spending time with him again. It reminded me just how much I had missed him. I'm not sure where it's going from here.''

''Where do you want it to go?''

She bit her lip. ''Good question.''

Alise fiddled absently with her chopsticks. ''It still blows me away that he was in a gang. Is he still, I don't know, into that?''

''I hope not. He gave me the impression that he wants to put all of that behind him.''

''Good for him.'' She took a sip of her soft drink. ''How did you two end up together in the first place?''

Rennie propped her chin on her palm.

"I was fourteen and he was sixteen when it began. Our relationship progressed slowly. After my brother's death, Gray stayed close to make sure I was okay."

"Because you were having trouble dealing with the loss?"

"That's an understatement. I went a little wild around that time. One night I showed up at the basement room where the gang used to hang out. I don't know what I was thinking. I made all kinds of threats and accusations. I basically yelled and screamed until I collapsed on the floor, weeping hysterically."

"Oh, Rennie."

"Gray got me out of there and took me home. He held me while I cried my eyes out. After that, he looked out for me, making it known on the streets that messing with me was messing with him."

"How romantic."

"Not at first. Most of the time he would

just walk me home from school and keep me company until I went to bed. I have no idea what he did after he left, but I know he didn't always go straight home.''

''Is that when he'd go hang with the rest of the gang?''

''I guess. It just killed me to know that he still had ties with the people who, I felt, were responsible for Jacob's death. It wasn't until I actually saw Gray with the gang that I tried to cut him off. He wouldn't let me shut him out, though.''

''What did he do?''

''He would follow me home even when I would try to run ahead. He would wait out front until I was safely inside my house. I went to great lengths to ditch him. The one time I was successful, I quickly regretted it.''

''Let me guess. You ran into trouble.''

Rennie nodded, dipping her California roll in soy sauce. ''Three boys from another school followed me that day. They were yelling dirty things and teasing me. When I got two blocks from my house, I wasn't sure if it was worse to lead them to my front door or risk getting cornered too far from home.''

''Rennie!'' Alise clutched both hands to her chest.

''I know. Luckily, Gray caught up with me and scared the kids off. I was so shaken up, I didn't even remember the walk home. Next thing I know I'm sitting in my living room and Gray is making me hot chocolate and trying to cheer me up with funny stories. After that, no matter how much I hated his involvement with the gang, I couldn't hate him.''

''Then I'm glad the two of you have found each other again. If you smoothed things over Friday night, what's the matter?''

''The problem is that I haven't heard

from him since then. I don't have any way to reach him except through the club. He doesn't have my numbers, either.''

''What about e-mail?''

Rennie rolled her eyes. ''You're not funny. We've just started to talk things out. I want to make sure he understands that I'm not judging him and that I'm will-ing to give him a chance.''

''If you need to get in touch with him, there's a solution,'' Alise said, looking pleased with herself.

Rennie leaned forward. ''What is it?''

''Call the club and ask if he's working tonight. If they say yes, go over there and talk to him.''

The last thing Rennie wanted was to ap-pear anxious. ''I don't know.''

Alise nodded. ''Don't wait around for him. You have to take control of the sit-uation. Do you want me to call Marlena so she can tell you the same thing with a lot more attitude?''

''That won't be necessary, but it's Sunday night. He's probably not working.''

''He might be. Sunday night is a big club night with college kids. You should go for it.''

Rennie sat still for a moment, thinking it over. ''You know, you're right. That's exactly what I'm going to do.''

Standing in front of Ocean, watching the neon sign blink on and off, Rennie began to reconsider whether coming here had been a good idea.

If possible, the line outside seemed twice as long as it had four nights ago. If she waited at the back, it would be after midnight before she got inside.

Deciding to take a chance, Rennie mustered her courage and marched to the front of the line. She wiggled through the crowd pushing against the velvet rope.

"Excuse me," she shouted, trying to get the attention of one of the bouncers. "I need to get inside."

He smirked. "Yeah, you and everybody else in line."

"No, I mean, I'm a friend of Gray's. I need to talk to him."

"Gray?" The bouncer studied her face very closely. Rennie stared at her shoes, embarrassed by the scrutiny. "Hey, do I know you?"

Rennie looked up, for the first time taking a good look at the bouncer she'd been talking to. A shiver darted down her spin. "N-no... I don't think so."

"What's your name?"

She tried to swallow past the dryness in her throat. "Rainbow," she said, her voice hoarse.

He stared at her for a few more seconds

then turned away. "Just a minute." He pulled a walkie-talkie off his belt loop and spoke into it while Rennie held her breath. A few seconds later he turned. "All right, come on."

"Me, too," shouted a blonde wearing blue-sparkled eyeshadow and pigtails. "I'm a friend of Gray's, too. He used to date my cousin."

The bouncer ignored the rowdy throng as others started shouting that they were friends of Gray. He pulled Rennie through the crowd and opened the rope for her. He led her inside and she pulled a ten-dollar bill out of her purse to pay her cover charge.

The man waved her off. "You're on the VIP list now. Your money's no good here. Wait here. He'll meet you by the door."

Rennie released the breath she'd been holding. Thank goodness he hadn't recognized her.

*   *   *

What was Rennie doing here? Gray
thought as he made his way to the front
of the club.

What if she ran into TK? He'd been
hanging around, and there was a chance
he still remembered Rennie.

It was best to keep their worlds as sep-
arate as possible. That was another good
reason for them not to see each other anymore. Unfortunately, the fact that they'd
slept together made things more difficult.
The last thing he wanted was for her to
feel as though he'd used her.

He walked up the stairs to the foyer and
saw Rennie huddling against a wall as
though she'd seen a ghost. His protective
instinct immediately kicked in. Was she in
trouble?

He rushed over. "Honey, what's
wrong? Are you okay?"

She looked around as though someone

might be watching her. "Can we go some-where more private?"

"Sure, come here." He took her to the VIP lounge. On Sunday nights the room was nearly empty. Not wanting to repeat the karma, he took her to the bar instead of a table.

"I wish you'd told me you were com-ing. I took my break early when I heard you were here, but I don't have much time. We've got a pretty rowdy private party in the Coral Dining Room, and I have to keep an eye on them."

"I don't want to take up much of your time. I just wanted to talk to you."

"What about?"

She chewed on her lower lip, looking distracted. "Can I ask you something else first?"

"Sure."

"I thought I just saw two of the guys you and Jacob used to run with. One of them was the guy who let me in here and the other was collecting money at the door. Was that my imagination?''

''No. Los and Woody work here.''

''You're still hanging out with your old gang? Do you think that's wise?''

Gray narrowed his eyes. He was in no mood to have this discussion with her. ''Doesn't everyone deserve a chance to do something better with their lives? I managed to find a pretty decent job, and I hooked up a couple of the boys from the old neighborhood. What's the big deal?''

''Well, if you're serious about getting your life together, it would probably help if you didn't surround yourself with people who put you on the wrong track to begin with.''

''What the hell is this? Did you come here just to lecture me on who my friends should be?''

Rennie looked stunned for a moment,

then she ran a hand over her face. "No, I'm sorry. I didn't mean to wax psychoanalytical on you. It just caught me off guard to see them here, that's all."

"So what *did* bring you here? Another night out with the girls?"

"No, uh, I hadn't heard from you, so I wanted to drop by and see how you were. It also occurred to me that you don't have my phone numbers." She reached into her purse and pulled out a card. "This has my home, work, cell, fax and e-mail...just in case."

"Look, I'm sorry I didn't get in touch with you yesterday. It's just that—"

"No, you don't have to explain. I just wanted to make sure that if you did want to contact me you knew how to reach me."

"Rennie, we'll talk. I promise. This just isn't a good time, okay? I'll call you."

She nodded, looking so vulnerable,

Gray felt his heart breaking for her. The situation was already a mess, and he hated to make it worse. Instead of giving her the gentle brush-off, he was making more promises.

"Look, about the other night. I didn't plan—"

"I know. Neither of us did. You don't think it was a mistake, do you?"

He took a beat too long to answer, and he saw her eyes begin to go glossy before she started blinking rapidly and staring at the floor.

"Why don't you go on home, okay, sweetheart? I get off duty around eleven. I'll call you then, okay?" He leaned down to kiss her cheek and said goodbye.

Why was this so hard?

He'd fought hand to hand with a Tae Kwon Do master during a drug bust in Tokyo. He'd run through the Kalahari Desert in South Africa with sharpshooters firing at him. He'd even jumped from a third story window into a moving vehicle. But nothing unnerved him more than seeing Rennie in pain.

TK watched Gray walk away from Rennie, and he smiled. He'd heard enough to know that some things never changed. Those two were still connected, and Gray still had one powerful weakness.

No matter what criminal activity went on in the back rooms of this club, he was still trying to play the hero.

Gray thought no one knew the real reason he joined their gang all those years ago, but TK wasn't stupid. Of course, he'd known. Rennie's brother, Jacob, wouldn't have lasted a day in the gang without Gray to back him up. But TK accepted them both because he'd thought he was getting a good deal. What little J had lacked in strength, he more than made up for in loyalty. And Gray had the muscle to get the job done.

Unfortunately, Gray also had a conscience, and it got in the way more times than TK cared to count. Little J would have done anything TK asked if Gray hadn't kept interfering. He was always stepping in with punk ideas that ultimately kept the gang from gaining any real juice.

With new Crips and Bloods gang sets popping up every day, taking over more territory, it had been hard for a small gang to make any money. He'd suggested they click up with the local Crips and get in on the real action.

Once again, Gray got in the way, convincing the others that they didn't want to get caught up in the Bloods and Crips gang war. He tried to convince them that they could make more loot while the Bloods and the Crips in their hood were busy fighting each other.

TK hadn't wanted to wait. He planned to live to be an O.G. Original Gangsters got all the respect, no matter what gang they ran with. He knew Gray would never last that long. He'd proven it when he promised them the juice and then he'd disappeared.

Now, all of a sudden, he was back, acting like a shot caller. He'd taken over, promising the old crew mad loot. They were TK's boys, his gang. It was his territory and he would have it back.

TK hated Gray. If he hadn't held them back, there was no telling where'd he'd be right now. He would love to take Gray out right now, but their gang law stood in his way. If one member turned on another, all the others would turn on him, and he'd be out in the cold.

TK had waited a lot of years, but he finally knew how to bring Gray down.

Gang code wouldn't let him challenge

Gray outright. Even though the old gang had fallen apart years ago, his men still lived by the code. They wouldn't follow him if he took Gray out. TK had to come in through the back door and take the operation out from under him.

And tonight, he finally found the key. If he couldn't get Gray directly, he'd get him through Rennie.

Chapter 6

Rennie was all set to turn in for the night when her telephone rang. "Hello."

"Hey, Rainbow."

"Gray." A warm heat spread through her chest at the sound of his voice. His call was right on time—just as he'd promised.

"You weren't asleep, were you?"

"No, I was still awake."

"I'm sorry we couldn't talk longer at the club—"

"No, don't worry about it. I didn't

mean to disturb you.'' Clearly, she'd over-reacted. If she'd been patient, he probably would have contacted her all by himself.

''Well, there is something that we should discuss.''

''Okay, but first, let me apologize for what I said about your co-workers. I should have realized that you were trying to help them.''

''Don't worry about that, but it does lead into what I wanted to talk to you about. I know you're having trouble understanding the turn my life has taken—''

''Gray, the only thing I need to know is that you're working on putting your life on the right track.''

''Believe me, Rennie, I am working on it. But, until I'm able to get on my feet again, maybe it would be best if we didn't see each other for a while.''

Rennie gripped the phone, not sure what to make of that statement. ''I can understand why you might feel that way. This has to be hard for you."

"Thanks, Rennie. I'm glad you can—"

"But you didn't let me shut you out of my life when Jacob died, and I don't plan to abandon you now. Even if you just need a friend, I want you to know that I'm here for you."

"I appreciate that, but things are more complicated than you realize."

"Do you want to explain it to me?"

He was silent for several moments. Finally, he said, "I need to stay focused on my goals. A relationship might be too much of a distraction in my life right now. Especially a relationship with you, Rainbow."

"What do you mean?"

"You're not just any woman to me. You deserve to have a man's full attention, and I can't promise you mine at this point."

"I'm not asking for anything from you, Gray."

"Honey, you don't have to ask. Just being with you makes me want to give it to you. You're not a casual fling kind of woman, and I'm not in a position to offer you much more than that."

"What if we agree to be friends for now? No pressure. I think we both could use that, don't you?"

Gray sighed, and Rennie held her breath, thinking he might disagree.

"Okay, Rainbow. Friendship it is."

Rennie hung up the phone, not really sure how she felt about their conversation. The most important thing was to be there for Gray. If he needed his life to be simple, then she had to respect that.

Seeing him again had stirred things up in her well-organized life. She could only imagine the commotion her presence was creating in his.

Because of Gray, Rennie had been thinking of her brother a lot more. Some of the memories were painful and some were sweet.

Rennie reached up and turned out the lights. Taking mental trips into her past had become a regular occurrence lately.

The day after Memorial Day in 1985 was the last time Rennie saw her brother alive.

After the festivities, Gray had spent the night at their house. The afternoon heat the following day had become so unseasonably humid, Rennie, Gray and Jacob decided to walk to the convenience store for ice cream.

Jacob strolled beside her with his usual casual grace in a white tank and baggy jeans. His shirt, sporting his gang colors, was wrapped around his waist. Gray followed them, wearing a white T-shirt with the sleeves ripped off and a pair of cutoff jeans.

The three of them were slowly rounding the corner, complaining about the escalating temperatures.

"This heat is ridiculous," Jacob said, tugging up the bottom of his tank to fan his stomach. "When I get home, I'm going to turn on all the cold water and bury myself in it in the bathtub."

"You do that, and Daddy will kill you for running up the water bill," Rennie warned him.

Jacob shook his head. "I don't care. It will be worth the butt-whooping just for a few minutes of relief from this heat."

Rennie shook her head, thinking nothing was worth one of daddy's belt whippings. She didn't receive them often, but she'd witnessed Jacob's lately. It was hard enough just to see him get them.

"Besides," her brother continued.

"Gray's going to get me a job with him waiting tables at Lino's Pizza. Then I'll be able to help out with the bills and Daddy won't be able to say jack to me. Isn't that right, Gray?"

"That's right. Mr. Kim is supposed to get back to me today. But I'm sure he'll hire you."

"Yeah, right. You know if Gray gets you a job, you aren't going to give it to Daddy for the bills. You're going to spend it all hanging out with your boys."

Jacob laughed. "Well, of course, I'm going to spend *some* of it on myself. What's the point of breaking my back working, if I can't enjoy it a little? But once I get a pair of new tennis shoes, a basketball and...well, a car, then Daddy can have the rest."

"I can't take it anymore," Gray said, groaning. "The gas station is a block over.

I'm going to run ahead and grab a soda. Anybody else want one?''

''Yeah, man, I'll take one.''

''Make mine orange,'' Rennie answered.

''Okay,'' Gray said, crossing the street. ''Y'all keep on, I'll catch up.''

Jacob and Rennie picked up the pace again. They were passing the park on the right when Jacob stopped dead in his tracks.

''That's TK and Woody over there.''

Rennie followed Jacob's gaze, and her heart sank. The two boys were scuffling with three other boys who were wearing rival gang colors.

She reached out to clutch Jacob's arm, trying to hold him back, but his elbow was already slipping through her fingers.

''Those aren't fair odds. I'd better go help them out.''

Rennie reached out again, grabbing a

fistful of his shirt. "Please, Jacob, stay out of it. This isn't your fight."

He scowled at her, trying to pull his shirt from her grip. "Of course it's my fight. If you step to one of my homies, you step to me. They'd jump in if they saw me getting jumped like that."

Rennie dropped her backpack and tried to hold on to Jacob with both hands. "Stay here. Or at least wait until Gray gets back so he can go with you."

Jacob pulled away, almost knocking Rennie off her feet. "Tell Gray what's going on when he gets back," he called over his shoulder.

Rennie twisted around, panic rising in her throat, hoping to see Gray coming up the street. There was no sign of him.

Abandoning her backpack on the sidewalk, Rennie moved closer, praying her brother wouldn't be hurt in the already nasty fistfight.

Jacob ran straight into the fray, grabbed one of the boys by the shoulder and started punching. The bigger kid stopped kicking TK, who was already down, and focused all of his attention on Jacob.

Rennie squeezed her eyes shut as her brother staggered back after the first blow. Again she started pacing the park, looking out for Gray.

When she turned, she saw another boy had started in on Jacob. While the two kids worked him over, Jacob did his best to deflect the blows. He was unsuccessful in landing any of his own.

Tears streaked down her face. She watched helplessly as her brother was beaten. Why weren't the other two boys helping him?

Feeling a hysterical urge to do something, Rennie searched for someone who could help her. Failing that, she looked around for a blunt object to use as a weapon. She had to do something to get those thugs off her brother.

As she turned, running from the park, she saw that Gray was headed up the street toward her. He took one look at her face, dropped the sodas and started running.

Rennie ran toward him, shouting that her brother was getting beaten up.

Gray started running full speed toward the park. He yelled for Rennie to stay where she was as he passed her.

Rennie immediately turned and followed him at a slower pace. Her vision was blurred with tears. Stopping at the opening of the fence, she dashed at her eyes with her arm.

"No!" Gray stopped running, calling out in a ragged voice.

Now that most of the focus was on her brother, TK had freed himself and was headed toward two of the rival gang boys with a broken pipe. At the last minute, the kid fighting Woody reached back and pulled a gun out of his jeans.

The gunman called a warning to his boys and they immediately scattered. Jacob came to his feet just in time to catch a bullet squarely in his chest.

Rennie stood frozen on the spot, unable to believe her eyes. Then she was screaming and running, somehow thinking she could get to Jacob before his body hit the ground.

He lay before her, a red stain growing on his white tank shirt. Blood covered her hands. Suddenly the park was empty except for Rennie and Gray.

Both of them stood in silence, crying over Jacob's lifeless body.

Rennie jerked upright in bed, her sleep shirt soaked through with sweat. Right after her brother had been killed, she'd relived that scene every night in her nightmares for weeks. It had been years since she'd had that awful dream.

Her body shaking violently, Rennie turned on her bedroom light and looked at the clock. It was just after three in the morning. Rennie climbed out of bed, stripped off her soaked nightshirt and pulled a fresh T-shirt from the drawer.

Her legs were barely steady enough to support her, and her breath was coming in rapid gasps. She reached up and touched her cheeks. They were wet with tears, and her throat was scratchy from screaming in her sleep.

The dream had been so real.

Rennie went to the kitchen and poured herself a glass of ice water to soothe her dry throat. She wasn't anxious to get back into bed right away, so she sat at the kitchen table.

Clearly, seeing Gray again brought back all her memories of her youth and her brother. Since they'd made love, she felt as if her life had shifted into some other dimension. One where she was intimately linked with him.

A small chill tingled her spine. At a moment like this, she really craved the comforting sound of his voice. She wished she had a way to contact him. Pride didn't matter right now. She knew in her heart that if he knew she needed him, he would be there for her.

Rennie stared at her frosty glass of water. Sometimes she missed her brother so desperately. He'd been a good person. Yes, for a while he allowed himself to get caught up in gang life, but that was only because he was searching for a place to fit in. At fourteen, Rennie had never run out of people to blame for her brother's death.

She blamed her father for working all the time and riding Jacob so hard on the few occasions they were together. She blamed herself for not finding the right words to talk him out of the gang. Sometimes she even blamed Gray, who had been nothing but a hero to her. But there were those times when she blamed him for not being fast enough or close enough to save her brother. She blamed Jacob himself for wanting to be the big man and for needing the makeshift family that the gang provided him with.

But when all was said and done, Rennie knew the only human being responsible for her brother's death was the boy who shot him. She'd come to terms with that fact years ago.

Remembering that incident in full detail reminded her that life was too short to let anything get in the way of important goals. Who knew how Gray was feeling after their unexpected encounter. Part of him may have decided to run away from the emotional intensity of their relationship. Perhaps he was ashamed of the time he spent in jail and didn't think he could face her.

Whatever his reasons were, Rennie knew she couldn't let him turn his back on what they had. Because for that brief instant when their bodies had been locked together, she knew they had seen into each other's souls. She'd never had such an experience with anyone since her first time with Gray, and she knew it was something she would never share with someone else.

If he didn't get in touch with her by tomorrow, she would call Ocean and see if they could get her in touch with him. She'd walked away from their relationship once. And she'd done it because of fear. Rennie had been afraid of the power and strength of their connection. She'd known if she wasn't careful it would consume her, come before everything she'd worked for, and she'd feared, eventually, she'd be trapped.

That was the real reason she left without saying goodbye. She'd known even then how strong her love for Gray was. And she knew that if he'd asked her, even in an unspoken request, to stay, she would have.

Now they had a second chance, and she could feel that everything they'd once shared was still present somewhere under the surface. She wouldn't let it go this time.

Even if Gray wanted her to. This time, she was going to see him through to the end.

Gray stared at the glowing green numbers flashing three thirty-six on his alarm clock. He'd been sitting on the edge of his bed, in the dark, staring at those numbers for what seemed like an eternity.

He'd thought of Jacob often over the years, but he couldn't remember the last time he'd had a dream about him that was so vivid and real. The dream shook him to the point that he woke up in a cold sweat, screaming…and missing Rennie.

He didn't know why, but he had the most powerful urge to see her. Speak to her. And not just because he knew she was the only person who would understand the dream. Even though she was the only one who could bring him comfort at that moment, he was more compelled by the feeling that she needed him.

It was ridiculous, he knew. It was the middle of the night. She had to work in the morning. Of course, while he was sitting up with the chills from a nightmare from his past, she would be sound asleep in the comfort of her bed.

Yet he still couldn't shake the feeling. If he weren't so certain she was asleep—

as anyone should be at 3:00 a.m.—he would have called her. He craved the sweet sexy sound of her voice.

It would have been nice to roll over and cling to her until her soft curves warmed the chill of his nightmare. Then slowly his sweaty panic would be replaced by a penetrating desire. Her hands, making slow, soothing circles on his back, would start rubbing and clutching at him with urgency, and they would make love, hot and sweet, until morning.

Gray blew out a harsh breath. Why was he torturing himself like this?

Just for the opportunity to distract himself from those stirring thoughts, Gray stalked toward the bathroom and ran cold water into the sink. He soaked his washcloth and mopped his face.

As Gray entered his bedroom, he let his mind wander to Jacob, seeing that bullet penetrate his chest over and over again in his mind's eye. It never should have happened. He should have been there to prevent it. Gray wasn't sure how he would have done it, but he was certain he should have tried. Even if it had meant taking the bullet himself.

Jacob had been the brother Gray had never had. He was an only child. Jacob had picked him out when they were in first grade and announced that Gray was going to be his best friend. He'd never said two words to the boy before that day, but from that afternoon forward, the two had been as close as real brothers. And Gray had Jacob's back no matter what trouble he managed to stir up for the two of them.

Gray hadn't been an angry or destructive kid—just a mischievous one, and when TK first approached Gray about joining his gang, Gray hadn't thought twice about turning down the offer. Jacob, on the other hand, hounded Gray to change his mind so they could both join.

Gray had refused, thinking if he didn't join, Jacob wouldn't, either. Unfortunately, Jacob hung around the gang members, finding ways to make himself indispensable to TK, until they asked him to join. At that point, Gray didn't have any choice. He had to join, as well, in order to keep Jacob out of serious trouble.

It didn't matter how many times he'd pulled Jacob's fat out of the fire or how many people he'd been able to save since. Even though, in the real world, he knew Jacob's death wasn't his responsibility, part of him would never be able to forgive himself for failing to save Jacob that night.

On good days, he could honestly say that he didn't let things affect him. But at times like this, everything piled up on him at once. It would have been nice to confide in Rennie. To share the weight of the burden he'd been shouldering on his own for so long. But that just wasn't possible now.

He didn't know how long it would take to smoke Simon out, and when everything went down, he couldn't predict how things would end. The possibility of dying hadn't meant much to him in the past. People died all the time. He grew up in a neighborhood where people never planned too far into the future because no one expected to live that long. Even now, he saw agents die every day. He took it for granted that one day it might be him.

Even if he could tell Rennie the truth, she wouldn't be able to live with odds like that.

For now, she wanted to be his friend. He couldn't make any reasonable arguments against that, but he knew it would be best for both of them if he kept his distance.

Eventually, she would come to agree with him.

*   *   *

"I know it's better that he's gone," Moni said. "But sometimes, in the morning, I'll wake up with this terrible sadness. It's like it comes out of nowhere. I'll think I've been getting over him just fine…and then *boom.* It hits me."

"Yes." Sarita spoke up. "That happened to me a lot after *mi vida* died. My mother, God rest her soul. I would dream about her and wake up crying. That still happens to me, and she died almost fifteen years ago."

Rennie nodded, identifying all too well with the feelings they were expressing. "Our worst fears come alive at night. Any of those things that we're worried, insecure or sad about. They run around in our minds when we sleep. When our minds are free from daily details like laundry or getting a baby-sitter."

"Well, I hate it," Moni said, punctuating her words by pounding on her thighs. "Because it means that I'm still not over him. And I want to be so badly."

"And you're getting closer, Moni. You can actually say Trey's name without a string of cusswords after it." Rennie laughed to keep the mood light, and the other women joined her.

"That's it for today, ladies. I'll see you all on Friday?"

"I won't be able to make it," Carla said. "Don's mother is coming for the weekend, and he wants me to play the happy homemaker deal."

All the women in the room froze, gaping at Carla.

"I know what you're thinking, and no, I resisted the urge to force-feed him the dish towel. I was tempted, but I remember what you said, Rennie, about letting him win sometimes. So he gets one home-cooked meal a day and a clean house while his mother's in town. Once she crosses back through the Seattle border, it's back to TV dinners and dust bunnies.''

Rennie smiled, because she knew for all of Carla's griping about her marriage, she really loved her husband, and through the help of the counseling sessions, she was learning to let go of the traumas of her childhood and actually express love openly.

"Okay, then I'll see everyone who's not entertaining in-laws, same time, same place, Friday.''

After her clients left her office, Rennie decided to stick around and catch up on some paperwork she'd been getting behind on.

The next time she looked at the clock,

it was nearly nine at night. She hadn't planned to get so swept up in her work.

As she stood up to stretch her tired muscles, she heard a noise coming from the hallway. She paused to listen more carefully. None of the other offices on this side of the building were open.

Was someone else working late, too?

Just then she heard the loud crash of something breaking. She listened for several more minutes, and when she didn't hear any footsteps, Rennie went to the door and peeked out.

Halfway down the hallway, Rennie saw that the decorative vase that sat on the table near the elevators had been broken. A large pile of colorful ceramic and dried flowers was scattered in the middle of the walkway.

Rennie sighed as she took in the mess. The day-care center was on that end of the hall, and all the kids would have to walk through the broken pottery when they arrived on Monday.

The janitorial staff usually worked in the evenings and had already left for the day. Rennie didn't want to run the risk of the heap sitting there all weekend.

The least she could do was sweep the shards under the table so the kids wouldn't have to come in contact with them.

Rennie knew she could find a broom and a dustpan in the supply closet at the end of the hall. She found the broom right away, but she had to hunt around for the dustpan.

Just as her fingers closed around it, Rennie heard footsteps in the corridor. "Is someone out there?"

As she moved toward the door, it slammed in her face, and the closet was plunged into darkness.

Chapter 7

Gray shoved the half-eaten burger on his plate away from him. "I'm not hungry anymore."

"Why not? You barely touched your food." Seth sat beside him at the diner counter.

He shook his head. "I think I just figured out why everyone in L.A. is so into bean sprouts."

Seth laughed. "Why is that?"

"Because no one around here knows how to make a decent burger. This thing is giving me indigestion,'' he said, clutching his stomach, which had begun to cramp.

''I had reservations for the Four Seasons tonight, but it seems they moved, leaving this cheesy greasy spoon in their place. Better luck next time.''

Gray stood, throwing some money on the counter. ''I've got to head out. The next time you have a message from Jonah, let's hit the hot dog vender. It's got to be better than this crap.''

As Gray got into his vehicle, he noticed that he still had that nagging pain in his stomach. He drove, and Rennie drifted into his mind.

On a whim, he turned his car around and headed toward her apartment. He knew he shouldn't try to see her, but he couldn't suppress his desire to talk to her.

When he didn't see her car parked outside her building, he should have gone on about his business, but something made him drive to her office instead.

Sure enough, Gray saw Rennie's car right away. What was she still doing there at this hour?

He entered the building, taking the time to read the directory to find out what floor her practice was on.

When he reached her office, he was surprised to discover that she wasn't inside. All the lights were on, her computer was running and her coat and bags were still there.

He waited around for several minutes, thinking she'd return from the ladies' room. When she didn't, he decided to take a look around.

All the offices on that floor were dark. He was about to head for the elevators when he heard a strange sound coming from the janitorial closet.

''Is anyone out there? Help! Help me!''

"Rennie? Hold on, honey, I'll get you out." He jerked open the door and she flew into his arms.

Gray tried to control Rennie's rolling, flailing body, but she wouldn't stop screaming and trying to strike out.

"Rennie! Rennie, it's me, Gray. Calm down, sweetheart. What's happened?"

Finally his voice seemed to penetrate her panic-stricken mind, and her body stilled. He helped her sit up, and her eyes seemed to focus on him for the first time.

"Gray! Thank God it's you." She wrapped her arms around him and held on for dear life.

He held her close, bringing her slowly to her feet. "What's going on, sweetheart?"

She pulled away and pointed toward the closet. "I think someone locked me in. I came looking for a broom and then I heard footsteps seconds before the door slammed shut.''

"Are you sure?" Gray moved to the door to inspect it. "Why would someone want to lock you inside?"

"I don't know, but I'm sure I heard someone walking around."

"The lock on this door is broken. Maybe someone walked by, and the breeze swept the door closed. The door could have easily locked on its own."

Rennie seemed to be calming down. "I suppose so."

"I'm sure that's what happened. Let's just get you home where you can feel safe."

They collected her things from her office, and Gray tucked her under his arm, walking her to his vehicle.

Her teeth had begun to chatter. "My c-car is over there."

"You can get it later. I'm going to drive

you home. You're too shaken up to drive right now.''

To his surprise, Rennie didn't put up an argument. In all the years he'd known her, he'd never seen her accept any authoritarian decision without at least commenting.

That proved how badly she'd been scared.

Gray helped Rennie into his car and headed for the highway feeling confused. Had someone intentionally locked her in that closet? It didn't make sense. Rennie didn't have any enemies.

He'd needed to help calm her down, but he was absolutely certain his first explanation was the answer. Once he had her comfortable and secure in her own home, he'd go back to the center and check things out, just to be sure.

All his senses were on alert, especially after running into TK. He didn't want to overreact, but it wouldn't hurt to look into all the possibilities.

Gray felt his gut twist. What if he *had* put Rennie in danger by reappearing in her life? He would never be able to forgive himself if that happened.

But, until he had more answers, he wasn't going to be able to stay away from her. If he discovered that she had been locked in that closet and was in some kind of danger, he would have to stick around and make sure she was protected. He could have Seth put a man on Rennie until everything settled down, but he wouldn't be able to sleep at night unless he personally saw to her safety.

Gray pulled up in front of Rennie's apartment and walked her into the building. Once inside, he got her curled up on the sofa while he found her something to eat.

After she'd finished, Rennie placed her

plate on the table and smiled at Gray. "Thank you so much for this. I didn't mean to be such a big baby. I hadn't realized until now that I'm a bit claustrophobic."

Gray studied her face. She looked much better. Her color had returned, and she was no longer shaky. Still, just to make sure she felt safe, he moved close and placed an arm around her shoulder. "Tell me what happened tonight."

"Well, I decided to catch up on some paperwork, and time sort of got away from me. Then I started hearing noises in the hallway."

Gray nodded, encouraging her to continue.

"There shouldn't have been anyone around at that late hour, so I took a peek into the hallway."

"Did you see anyone out there?"

Rennie pressed a hand to her forehead.

"No, but I saw a broken vase lying in the middle of the walkway. Since it happened so close to the day-care center, and the kids usually come in early in the morning, I went to the supply closet for a broom. You know the rest."

Gray nodded, taking a deep breath. The important thing was that Rennie was safe. His job was to make sure she stayed that way.

The two of them lapsed into silence. Gray started to think about how he could take care of his work at Ocean and keep an eye on Rennie. He glanced over at her and saw a small wrinkle between her brows.

He squeezed her shoulder, made slow circles on her upper arm. "Are you alright now, sweetheart?"

She nodded. "Yes, having you here helps a lot. What brought you to the center, anyway?"

What had brought him to the center? All he knew was that he'd had to see her. ''I guess I needed someone to talk to, after all. Being friends with you is going to take some…adjustment.''

Rennie gave him a wry smile. ''I know that it's complicated.''

''You can say that again.''

''I don't think either one of us was expecting what happened between us the last time.''

''Yeah, I guess we need to talk about that.''

''We can talk about it if you want, but there's something you ought to know.''

''Whoa, that sounds heavy. You can't be pregnant already, besides the fact that we used protection. What put that serious note in your voice?''

''I'm serious about what I'm about to say. I know the temptation right now would be to walk away. Chalk the other night up to reminiscing and keep all of this in the past. But I'm not going to let either of us do that. I think it's time for both of us to stay and face what's going on between us, complicated or not.''

Gray laughed, partly because it scared him how well she could read his mind after all this time. And partly because she had no idea how much she sounded like a shrink.

''So are you planning to practice your psychoanalysis on me?''

Her brow furrowed. ''What do you mean?''

''Well, it sounds like you're all set to launch into one of your counseling sessions. Talking about how we're going to face our feelings and such.''

Rennie released a nervous laugh. ''Oh, hazard of the job. A close friend of mine is a lawyer and she can't resist the urge to cross-examine her friends when we're not dishing the dirt fast enough. I guess I do tend to use the psychobabble when I really care about something.''

Gray began to feel flirtatious. A simple emotion he hadn't experienced in quite a while. ''Ah, is that your way of telling me you care about me?''

Rennie went coy, lowering her lashes and watching him through them. ''Maybe…maybe not.''

''Well, what's it going to take to make up your mind?'' He leaned over until his breath stirred the hairs on her neck.

''That depends. What have you got?''

He chuckled, watching the tiny hairs dance on a ripple of air. ''Let's see. I've got a little of this.'' He pressed his lips to the nape of her neck and nibbled. Rennie used to wear her hair in a ponytail when they were kids. She'd loved it when he would kiss her neck directly below the knot of her hair.

Now her hair was short and stylish, the way many fashionable women wore it these days. It was cropped just above that special place he'd always kissed.

After placing several light kisses on that spot, he raised his lips to her earlobe, her second favorite spot. "And I've got a little of this."

"Hey, watch the earrings," Rennie joked. "They were very expensive."

"Give me your hand."

"Why?"

"Just give me your hand."

When she didn't respond right away, Gray reached down and took her hand, raising her open palm toward his mouth. He placed a gentle kiss on her palm, leaving her gold stud in the center.

Rennie closed her palm around the earring, shaking her head. "Cute."

He chuckled. "Thanks. I look even better with a fresh shave.'' He rubbed his stubbled jaw playfully.

''I didn't mean you, silly.''

''You didn't?'' He pretended to pout. ''Does that mean you don't think I'm cute?''

She studied his face. ''I don't think cute is the right word. I think sexy suits you better.''

Gray bobbed his eyebrows lasciviously. ''Ooh, baby, keep talking.''

And then he covered her lips with his.

''How can I...talk when you're... kissing me?'' she muttered against his lips.

He pulled away just long enough to utter, ''Okay, I take it back. Shut up.''

Then he pressed his mouth over hers again, parting her lips and gently gliding his tongue into her mouth. Rennie responded eagerly, touching her tongue to his before she slanted her mouth more to allow a deeper kiss.

As the kiss began to get hot, Gray pulled away. "Is this your idea of friendship? Because I think this is indicative of a bit more than that."

Rennie tugged his head back down to hers. "Who cares? Stop talking."

No one had to tell him twice. He let Rennie resume their kiss, and suddenly things were spiraling out of control. Their mouths were hungry on each other. Lips, teeth, tongues.

Their hands were everywhere. Touching, grasping, rubbing. Their clothes were only half off when Gray sheathed himself and entered her. They were both so desperate for the connection, neither wanted to wait to stop completely.

As soon as Gray felt Rennie's warm, tight softness, he groaned. "Rennie, oh, honey…"

Rennie's nails dug into Gray's back as their bodies rocked together and apart. Together and apart. Then she was pulling away. "Let me be on top."

Gray sat up on the couch, keeping their bodies fused as he picked her up and settled her on his lap. "Oh, yeah, I like that," he whispered, watching Rennie's half naked body arch above his.

Bracing her hands on his shoulders, Rennie lifted and lowered her body on his. Gray guided her hips with his hands until the sight of her naked breast bobbing before him was too much.

He reached up, cupping both breasts in his palms. Pausing her motions while he suckled her.

Then she was moving again, keeping close eye contact with him as she worked her body on his. Gray threw back his head, letting the sensations escalate inside him. "That's it, baby. Yes."

Lifting his head, Gray watched Rennie. He loved the look of pure feminine power in her eyes. It really turned him on.

He began to feel himself losing control. Gripping her hips tightly, he stilled her movements, quickly flipping her beneath him.

He drove his body forcefully into hers again and again as Rennie clung to him, making sweet, pleasured sounds.

Later, in bed, Rennie rolled over to find Gray watching her. The expression on his face was so intense, it startled her.

"What's on your mind?" she asked, reaching out to stroke his bristled cheek.

He opened his mouth, but she cut him off. "Don't you dare say *nothing*."

Gray rolled away from her watching gaze to lie on his back. "Sometimes I'm just surprised to wake up and find myself here."

She thought she already knew the answer to her next question, but she couldn't keep herself from asking it anyway. "Is that a good thing, or a bad thing?"

To her surprise his response was not immediate.

"It's a good thing."

"But..." She prodded.

"But I'm not sure I'm at a place in my life where this—" he motioned to the two of them "—is a good idea."

Rennie nodded, letting his words sink in. "Is that because you spent time in prison?"

She watched Gray carefully, seeing him flinch.

His lips tightened. "Maybe. Partially."

"Why?"

He turned onto his side, facing her. "Rennie, being with you here, like this, sometimes I can forget. Sometimes I can pretend that I'm the same person who was

in love with you years ago. But the fact
is, I'm nothing like the person you remember.''

She looked at him, noticing that the
smooth lines of his face were harder, that
he had a darkness in his eyes that hadn't
been there years ago. She'd seen gang life
consume her brother. It had hardened and
desensitized him and finally it killed him.

All the years she'd been away, she'd
prayed that Gray had made it out—just
like they'd talked and dreamed about so
many nights on her living room floor. It
had broken her heart when she'd been told
he was arrested.

His eyes held the kind of age only hard
knocks could bring, but she'd swear she
still saw traces of the boy she used to
know. In the way his eyes softened when
he looked at her. And in the way his lips
tilted at the corners instead of a full smile.

''I know that. I don't expect you to be

the same person you were back then. *I'm* not even the same person I was. It's true that it's easy to get caught up in what was a reality nine years ago. But the fact is we need to get to know each other as we are now. Are you willing to do that?''

Gray was silent for several minutes, and Rennie knew that this wasn't a good time to push him for an answer.

When he finally did speak, his eyes had taken on a hardness she'd never seen before. ''Rennie, I'm not sure you'd like the person I am now. I may need some time to find out exactly who that is.''

Rennie could no longer hold back the urge to touch him. She reached out and let her index finger stroke gently over his arm. ''I know you've gone through a lot in the time we were apart. I know you made some mistakes. And when you're ready to talk about that part of your life,

I want you to know that I'll listen without judging you.''

Gray tried to interrupt her, and she stopped him.

''Just let me finish. What you don't seem to know is that I know your soul. I remember parts of you that you've forgotten, and that's okay. Because the changes that you've gone through couldn't have changed the good person I know you to be. Maybe you just need someone to remind you that person is still in there.''

''Rennie—''

''I know, I know...you think this is a bunch of my psychobabble again, but it's not. I mean it. I can feel you in here.'' She pointed to her chest. ''Still, after all this time, as though you've never left. And do you know why that is?''

Gray lifted a shoulder in question. ''Why?''

''Because you didn't. You never left.

As far apart in time and geography as we've been, I've always kept you in my heart.''

Gray was quiet, but Rennie could see that her words were moving him. Not wanting to push too hard, she tried to change the topic.

''Thanksgiving is on Thursday. Do you have any plans?''

''Not really. I haven't been in the habit of celebrating that holiday for years.''

Rennie fiddled with the corner of her pillowcase, surprised by the butterflies that had suddenly appeared in her stomach.

''Would you like to spend the holiday with me?''

He smiled at her. ''Rennie, that holiday is for family. You should be with yours.''

She looked at her hands. ''I don't really have any family left. I'm not sure if you know that my father died during my junior year in college.''

"Rennie, I'm sorry."

"Thanks. After I left for school, I kept calling home to make plans to visit. Dad would always make me cancel, saying that he was picking up an extra shift or that he was too tired to be good company. He couldn't find the time to visit me, either. We did speak on the phone, though. That was probably the closest we'd ever been."

Gray rubbed comforting circles on Rennie's back. She looked at him. "I also heard about your mom. Seems like you're in the same boat I am when it comes to family."

Gray nodded. "Looks like you and I are the closest thing to family either of us has left."

"That's right. So we have to spend this holiday together."

"I would love to spend Thanksgiving with you."

"Great, I'll cook."

"On second thought—"

Rennie punched him in the arm, making him howl.

"Just kidding, Rainbow. I'm looking forward to it."

Chapter 8

Rennie stared at the oven timer with rising anxiety as it ticked off each second. This was her first time preparing Thanksgiving dinner, and everything had to be perfect. Unfortunately, she was beginning to suspect her special meal was going to be anything but.

She'd thought she was being so clever when she decided not to prepare an entire turkey for herself and Gray. Instead Rennie used the gourmet recipe for stuffed turkey breasts that she saw on the cover

of a magazine in the grocery check-
out line.

She flicked on the oven light and peered
through the window once more. The two
awkward lumps of turkey, with stuffing
exploding from every crevice, in no way
resembled the glossy magazine picture.
But she'd followed every step to the letter,
so it was still possible that all the magic
was in the baking.

Turning from the oven, Rennie resumed
chopping vegetables for the salad. She'd
had to stop twice to retrieve Band-Aids,
but she'd never considered herself the do-
mestic type, anyway.

Yet, despite the minor glitches Rennie
had encountered so far, she couldn't help
basking in the new sensations that were
greeting her. It felt so good to be cooking
for Gray. That alone was surprising
enough, because Rennie didn't much care
for cooking, which was why her refriger-

ator was perpetually empty. She kept the fridge at the center better stocked than she kept the one in her own home.

Rennie cooked just enough not to starve, and she was certain that it was she alone keeping the microwave dinner manufacturers in business. But preparing this meal for Gray was different. And it wasn't just the holiday, although that was significant, too—they were spending an occasion reserved for families *together*. In a way, that made them family. Gray and Rennie. She liked the sound of that.

Still, the real reason Rennie was enjoying cooking for Gray was it gave her the opportunity to do something special for him. Gray had spent a lot of time taking care of others. It wasn't often that anyone had taken the time to take care of him.

Besides, if this meal turned out well, she might even grow to like cooking.

At her fantasy of their special dinner,

Rennie nicked herself with the knife for the third time that night. Cursing as she bandaged her thumb, she was almost relieved to hear the phone ringing.

"Hello?"

"I knew it! I *knew* you were lying," Marlena shouted into Rennie's ear, causing her to fumble with the phone. When she finally got the receiver to her ear, Marlena was in full swing.

"Get your things together, Ren. I'll be there in fifteen minutes."

"Here? Fifteen minutes? What are you talking about?"

"Don't argue. You're coming with me to my parents'. I gave them a heads-up that I might bring you when you gave me that cock-and-bull story about having dinner with some friends of the family. Admit it, you're there alone, aren't you?"

"Yes, right now, but—"

"There's no way I'm letting you spend

the holiday on your own. I'll be there in ten.'' Click.

For one stunned moment, Rennie didn't move. Then she sprang to life and punched out Marlena's number on the phone. When her friend was on the line, Rennie didn't give her a chance talk.

''Listen. You were right. I'm not having dinner with some friends of the family tonight—''

''I knew it. I knew it. Alise owes me twenty bucks. I told her that you don't have any family, so how could they possibly have any friends?''

Rennie kept talking. ''The truth is it's only *one* friend of the family. Gray's going to be here in less than an hour.''

Marlena's end was so quiet, for a moment Rennie feared her friend had hung up and was already halfway to her house. Then she heard the uneven rushes of air that indicated Marlena was still there and breathing into the line. Wow, she must have stunned her speechless.

In the year she and Marlena had been friends, Rennie had never seen the woman at a loss for words.

Finally, Marlena released a sound between a sigh and a croak. "You're having dinner with Gray. No, you're having *Thanksgiving* dinner with Gray? When did all this happen? I thought you hadn't seen him since that night Alise talked you into going after him at the club. Have you two started up again and why didn't you tell me?" If Rennie didn't know better, she'd swear Marlena sounded a bit hurt.

"I'm not sure where this is going yet. You know, things kinda moved forward before we could really analyze what was happening."

"Are you kidding me? You analyze everything."

"I know. I think I may already be in over my head."

"What happened? I want to know everything."

"It's a long story. We'll have to get together for drinks after work some time next week. I'll catch you up on all the details."

"So...who's cooking?"

"I am," she said proudly.

"Well, this must be serious for you to brave the wild jungle of pots and pans for him."

Rennie carried the cordless into the kitchen and lifted the lid of the ceramic casserole dish she purchased just for this occasion. "Can I ask you something?"

"Anything."

"Are sweet potatoes supposed to be crusty?"

"I don't know. What did you put on them?"

''The recipe said I should sprinkle them with brown sugar and let them sit for awhile. I don't know. Right now they look like I left them out in the rain and they rusted.''

''Eew, that sounds nasty. I hope Ocean has a good health plan. Do you want my advice?''

Rennie thought about it for a minute. Marlena was only slightly more skilled than Rennie in the kitchen...and that was because she brewed her coffee in a pot instead of using instant. ''If you tell me to order take-out—''

''No, I'm serious. Mom makes sweet potatoes every year, and believe it or not, I've actually been known to help a time or two. There's only one way to save that mess you've got there. Add some butter and cinnamon and serve them mashed.''

''Mashed sweet potatoes? Really?''

''It's either that or buy a premade crust and make pie filling out of it.''

''Thanks, I'll try mashing them first.''

''You know, if things aren't working out in the kitchen, you can still come to Mom and Pop's with me. I might even let you bring Gray.''

''Thanks, Marlena, but I think I'll be okay. I might get the hang of this cooking thing yet.''

Rennie hung up the phone and did her best to salvage the sweet potatoes. By the time she'd mashed them and added butter and cinnamon, they were looking pretty edible. She'd just covered them with plastic wrap when the oven timer went off.

Crossing her fingers inside the oven mitt, Rennie removed her stuffed turkey breasts. She released a weary sigh as she studied the contents of the pan.

''Well, maybe it will look better after

I've sliced it,'' she muttered, taking a carving knife from the drawer.

By the time the doorbell rang, Rennie had restored order to her kitchen. She checked her hair in the reflection of the microwave oven. And looked over her long denim skirt and lavender sweater to make sure there were no food stains on them.

Several covered dishes were warming on the stove. Rennie walked to the door feeling confident that Gray would never know she'd had to change both her clothes and the menu twice.

Gray walked into Rennie's apartment with a pumpkin pie in one hand and a bottle of wine in the other. ''Mmm, everything smells great.''

''Thanks.'' Rennie took the pie from him and gave him a soft kiss on the lips.

''Everything is ready. If you want to pour the wine, I'll set the table.''

Gray went into the kitchen for a corkscrew. As he filled Rennie's glass, he automatically questioned whether he should offer her the standard excuse for why he couldn't join her in drinking. Technically, he was still on duty.

A swell of resentment rose up, crashing over his chest like a breaking wave. When in the last five years had he *not* been on duty?

He poured himself a glass. Didn't he deserve a night off? Sure, bouncing straight from one assignment to the next, never long out of active duty had been his choice. It had made up for the fact that he hadn't created a real life for himself, and masked the fact that he had no friends, no family, no lover to return home to.

He hadn't played it strictly by the book. Gray had had his share of affairs, however fleeting. But he'd always made it clear he'd be moving on soon, so he hadn't needed to deal with commitments or emotional involvement.

But things were different with Rennie. He'd been emotionally involved with her for the past nine years, even though he hadn't once laid eyes on her. She was the mistress he carried in his heart, preventing him from giving any other woman more than his body.

Gray took a deliberate sip from his glass. Yes, he deserved a night off. Simon wouldn't move tonight. Gray's men were taking care of all the details at the club. The world wouldn't end if he lived for himself just once.

Rennie appeared in the kitchen doorway. "Are you going to stand here sipping wine all night, or are you going to join me at the table?"

"Sorry. Just making sure I didn't bring

a wine that was too dry for you. I know you prefer it sweet,'' he said, following her out of the kitchen.

They sat down at the table and Gray served them both from each dish. ''Everything looks delicious.'' He started to stick his fork into the mashed sweet potatoes.

''Do you want to say grace, or shall I?''

Gray's fork clattered to the plate as his face heated. ''Uh, why don't you say it this time.''

He bowed his head as Rennie said the prayer. When it was over, he said, ''I didn't realize you were religious.''

Rennie took a bite of her food, relief clear on her face. ''Not as much as I'd like to be, but this is Thanksgiving, and lately I've had so much to be thankful for.'' She gave Gray a meaningful look.

If she knew the truth, Rennie would be anything but thankful for his presence in her life. Feeling a stab of guilt, he looked away.

His discomfort must have been more obvious than he'd realized, because Rennie rushed to speak, "I meant that I'm thankful for not ruining this meal. You know I've never been anyone's Julia Child."

"You did great. I've never had turkey casserole before, but it's delicious." She'd clearly gone to a lot of trouble for him, when all he could offer in return was poor company and lies. He didn't know how to do this anymore. How to be a regular guy. How to make small talk without a hidden agenda.

Spending Thanksgiving with Rennie had obviously been a mistake. She would have been better off surrounded by her friends, eating a meal with a real family who knew how to make her feel welcome.

"Are the sweet potatoes too sugary?"

"No, they're fine. Perfect."

"Okay. For a minute there I was afraid they'd inadvertently glued your lips closed. You haven't said more than two words since you got here."

Gray looked at Rennie. She looked so beautiful and she'd gone to so much trouble, and here he was making a mess of things. "I'm sorry, Rainbow. I've just got a lot on my mind."

Rennie nodded and continued poking at her dinner. Finally, she said, "Well, I know there's one less worry on my mind."

"What's that?"

"All the locks were checked at the center yesterday. The closet I was stuck in and few other old locks were totally replaced. It's a relief to know something like that won't be happening again."

"So they decided that it was definitely a faulty lock and not an intruder."

"Yes. The building showed no signs of breaking and entering. It feels good to have that confirmed. I think I'd been getting a little paranoid."

Gray stilled. "What do you mean?"

"Well, I think I psyched myself out. For the past few days I've had the creepy sensation that I was being watched or followed. I know it's crazy, but it also doesn't help that Mrs. Scarphelli from upstairs had her car broken into right outside in the parking lot. Maybe I've been watching too many suspense movies."

"You felt like you were being watched? When was this? Where were you?"

"I'm sure it was nothing."

He wasn't so sure about that. "Tell me anyway."

"Gray, I didn't tell you about this to get you upset. I told you so you *wouldn't* worry."

"I'm glad that they got everything

taken care of at the center, but one thing may not be related to the other. You don't work in the safest part of the city, Rennie. Just tell me what made you think you were being watched.''

Rennie sighed and put her fork down. ''You're going to think I'm being silly.''

''No, I won't. Just tell me.''

''Okay, well, the other day I stopped at the grocery store to pick up a few things. There was a man who seemed to be following me, putting all the same things in his basket that I was choosing.''

''A man? What did he look like.''

''It doesn't matter because as it turns out, it was just a silly coincidence. After the third time it happened, I stopped and looked at him. He laughed and commented on our similar taste. Then I started to think he was trying to hit on me, but he turned and walked away.''

''What did he look like?''

"I don't know. He was African American, average height. You know, regular-looking. It was nothing, though. I never saw him again. I got worked up for no reason."

Gray nodded silently. It was obvious the man who was following Rennie wasn't TK, but Gray wasn't so sure it wasn't someone who worked with him.

"Did anything else unusual happen?"

"Not really. Just stupid things. Like being sure someone was staring at me, but when I turned around there wasn't anything unusual going on."

"What do you mean? When you turned around the street was empty? Or when you turned around no one was looking at you?"

"The second one. You know, I would just see regular people on their way into a diner or talking to a street vendor. Nothing. Just my own paranoia."

Gray nodded, making the motions of eating dinner. He didn't touch his wine again. His head needed to stay clear. If TK was watching Rennie. He had to know why.

He slipped his hand under the table and used the tine of his fork to depress a hidden button on his pager. Right now a signal was being sent to Seth Greene's pager.

Rennie had just cleared the dinner dishes and was placing the pie on the table when Gray's pager vibrated, letting him know that Seth was in place.

"Rennie, before we have dessert, I need to run out to the store."

She frowned. "For what?"

"A pack of cigarettes."

"You still smoke?" Rennie used to become furious with him when they were kids and she would catch him smoking. He'd learned never to do it in front of her, but still she'd known and had nagged him relentlessly about it.

"Yes, and I know you don't like it, but I've been doing it for too long to quit now."

Rennie nodded toward the window that was being pelted with heavy rain. "You're going to go out in the middle of a rainstorm just to have a cigarette."

Gray was already halfway out the door. "I won't be long, I promise."

He ran three blocks to a newspaper vendor on the corner. Seth stood behind the counter waiting for him. "Can I get you something?" he asked with a grin.

Gray was in no mood to play along. His shoes were squishing and his socks were sopping wet. "Did you get anything new on TK?"

"Nothing new. Why? Has he made a move?"

"I think he's watching Rennie."

"Rennie? Your old high school girl-friend?"

"Yes. Not only has she had the feeling that she's being followed, she got locked in a closet after hours at the Help Center. I don't think it's a coincidence."

Seth nodded. "Probably not."

"I want put a man on her. If one of TK's men is tailing her, I want one of our guys watching him follow her."

Seth scratched his chin. "I don't know...."

"What's to know? How soon can we get this done?"

"Uh, Gray...this sounds like a personal issue. I don't know if SPEAR will go for using a man to protect your girlfriend. You know Jonah wants all of our man-power focused on Simon right now. Maybe if it were directly related to the mission..."

"It *is* related to the mission. If TK is

on to Rennie, it's because of me.'' Gray pulled his trench coat tighter around him, trying to block the rain that was hammering on his back. ''Look, you're going to have to trust me on this one. No doubt, it's some kind of warning. TK lives by the old code. If he wants me out of the way, he's not going to take me down directly.

''One thing you learn in prison is how to get to your enemies. You can't just walk up and stab someone with a fork without getting sent to the hole. You have to learn how to play with their minds. I think that's what TK is doing. Trying to get at me through Rennie. When I'm not looking he's going to try to break in on everything I've been working for.''

Seth nodded. ''I hear what your saying, but it's going to be a tough sell. I'll see what I can do. In the meantime, try to keep an eye on her yourself. If you get something more solid than a hunch, then I might be able swing it.''

Gray nodded, getting a sickening, sinking feeling in the pit of his stomach. They spoke for a few more minutes before Gray turned and ran into the rain.

He might not be able to prove it, but he was sure that TK was up to something. The only way to protect Rennie was to get this mission done and get out of her life. He'd see what he could do about speeding up the process with Simon. Meanwhile he'd stick close to Rennie.

Rennie stacked the last of the dirty dishes in the dishwasher and slammed the door closed. After all the trouble she'd gone to, Thanksgiving dinner had been a big fat flop. Oh, the meal had been a success, but she and Gray had barely spoken. He sat across from her with that brooding look on his face.

Then, rather than share the pumpkin pie and warm apple cider she'd prepared, he preferred to run out into the rain for some stinking cigarettes.

Rennie was so angry, she could barely sit still. She hoped Gray wouldn't even bother to come back. No, she hoped he would come back and find *her* gone.

She sank into the sofa cushions, hugging a throw pillow to her chest. Where could she go? She couldn't think of a single place to go this late on a holiday in the pouring rain. So she decided to do the next best thing.

It would serve him right to come back and find her in her pajamas with the lights out. Of course, that might be more inviting than discouraging. Her thoughts drifted in a different direction, and she felt herself blush.

There would be none of that tonight. She wouldn't even take the chain off the door, Rennie decided. She'd let him see that she was dressed to sleep—alone—in her nightwear, and tell him to go on home.

Set in her resolve, Rennie was in the midst of turning out the lights when she heard knocking at the door. Still feeling pouty and not caring how childish she appeared, Rennie trudged to the door and peeked through a narrow sliver.

"You know, Gray, I'm tired and I think I'll just—"

Rennie was stunned speechless when Gray held up a bouquet of red roses. She flung the door wide open.

Gray held the roses out as he gave Rennie a one-armed hug.

"I'm sorry, Rainbow. I know I was a jerk tonight. The flowers are an apology. Sorry, they're kinda wet."

"Oh, my goodness, thank you."

Rennie put them in a glass vase from the kitchen. When she returned, Gray had taken off his wet coat and shoes and was reclining on the sofa.

He sat up when she entered the room. ''Sweetheart, I'm sorry for how I was acting. It's been a long time since I've celebrated holidays or any special occasions. I think this whole thing has sort of caught me off guard.''

Rennie was immediately overwhelmed with guilt.

She'd been so busy trying to make this a special dinner for him, she'd forgotten how much this would remind him of all the dinners that weren't special in his lifetime.

Had he spent his last Thanksgiving in prison?

She wanted desperately to ask him. But she had to fight her natural instinct to dissect and analyze. Some things were better expressed without words.

So she walked over and sank down next

to him on the couch. He scooted over to give her room, and Rennie wrapped her arms around his neck.

Gray returned her hug warmly.

"So, what were you about to say when you opened the door?"

"Uh, that I was going to bed, but—"

He cut her off with a finger over her lips. "No, don't let me change your plans."

He stood, keeping her pinned to his side. "If you're ready for bed, so am I. On a night like tonight, the best place to be is snuggling under the covers."

Chapter 9

TK lurked among the Christmas shoppers, watching Rennie and her friend Sarita. Because of the dense holiday crowd he was able to stand as close as he liked without being seen. It gave him a rush to know that he could do whatever he wanted to Rennie Williams and then melt into the crowd before anyone identified him.

He laughed to himself as the two women stopped at a mall cart that sold colorful wrapping paper. His plans were coming together. That woman had no idea what was going on. Her life was returning to normal, and she was starting to feel safe again.

He'd seen the way she acted after he locked her in that closet. She couldn't go anywhere without looking over her shoulder. He bet she had felt tingles on the back of her neck even when his boys weren't brushing up against her on the street or following her in the grocery store.

And she'd reacted exactly the way he'd expected her to. She'd run straight into Gray's arms for comfort. TK released another deep laugh from his gut. And in the meantime, he'd started hanging out with a few of the boys from the old gang. No big deal. Just catching a drink every now and then.

He was slowly reminding them what life was like when he ran the show. Subtly hinting that things could be like that again. He didn't mention Gray at all. It was too soon. Once things started getting too hot for Rennie, Gray would start falling apart all on his own.

And when the boys started to feel like they were only getting half of Gray's attention, when they started to realize that Gray's personal life might be interfering with their cash flow, then TK would be there with a plan of his own.

He watched as Rennie and Sarita laughed and talked, filling their shopping bags with all the trappings of Christmas. The holiday season had lifted her spirits. Made her feel comfortable again. After all, 'tis the season to be jolly. Right?

TK continued to laugh as he turned away and disappeared into the crowd. He'd seen enough. It was time rock Rennie's safe little world.

Rennie smiled at Sarita as she sat across from her in the tiny mall café that was crowded with holiday shoppers. "Sounds like you and Los are pretty serious."

Sarita grinned. "I'm working on it. Right now, my biggest problem is that we don't spend enough time together."

"I can understand that. Between school and working at the hospital, it must be hard to—"

"That really isn't the problem. It's Ocean."

"Ocean? Don't you all spend time together on the nights you sing there?"

Sarita shook her head. "Those are the nights I *don't* see him. He's so busy all the time."

"I thought he was a bouncer, like Gray."

"He is, but I don't think that's all they do there," she said bitterly, then caught herself.

"What do you mean?"

Sarita was quiet for several minutes before she shrugged and looked away. "I don't know. It just takes up more of his time than I expected. So how are things with you and Gray?"

Rennie sucked in a deep breath. She had to learn to let her guard down a bit more. It was still so difficult for her to discuss her personal life with Sarita. After all, she was a client. But they had also become friends. The men they were dating worked together, so it was likely they would see more of each other outside the Help Center.

"Not bad. We've been spending a lot of time together lately. It's strange because at times it's like being with someone who knows me better than I know myself. Then there are other times when I feel like I'm getting to know someone completely new."

"Which feeling do you like better?"

Rennie smiled. "I like both. It keeps

things interesting. I guess I can relate to what you said about the time issue, though. It seems the only time we can spend together is in the evenings, before he goes to work at the club.''

Sarita rubbed her chin. ''I wonder what they're up to?''

''What do you mean?'' That was the second time Sarita had made a strange comment. She spent a lot more time at the club than Rennie did. Did she know something she didn't want to tell Rennie? Could Gray be in trouble again?

''Nothing. I mean who can understand how the male mind works? You're a shrink, Rennie, and even you don't know. Otherwise, maybe you'd be working with men instead of just women, right?''

''That's true. Men don't view the world from the same perspective as women, but are you sure that's what you were talking about?''

"Of course. I mean, why would our men prefer to spend time in a smoky nightclub when they could be spending quality time with sophisticated women like us? They'd better not be picking up any hoochie mamas in tight skirts."

Rennie laughed. "I'm sure Los wouldn't dare."

"What about Gray?"

Rennie didn't even pause to consider the possibility. She knew she could trust him. "*He* wouldn't dare, either."

The two of them finished their coffee and decided to head home. Rennie gave Sarita a lift to her car. Before she got out, Sarita paused. "What kind of car does Gray drive, Rennie?" she asked.

Rennie paused, trying to call up a picture in her mind. She shook her head. "I can't remember the brand, but it's one of those sport utility vehicles. Something black. Why?"

Sarita shrugged. "Just curious. Los drives a BMW Z3."

"Wow. That's a nice car," Rennie said, to be polite.

She wasn't really sure what point Sarita was trying to make. The woman hadn't struck her as the type to date a man based on the car he drove.

"Yeah, it is a nice car. Very nice...for a bouncer."

A cold wave of realization washed over Rennie. Before she could say another word, Sarita closed the car door and got behind the wheel of her Dodge Charger.

Rennie continued to sit in the car after Sarita pulled out of the space and drove away. Slowly, Rennie inched forward, caught up in Sarita's parting words. Suddenly, all Sarita's earlier comments made more sense. Clearly, Sarita suspected that Los might be involved in some kind of illegal activity in addition to his work at Ocean.

How else would he be able to afford to drive such an expensive car? Rennie shook her head in dismay. Why hadn't she picked up on this sooner? Of course, Sarita hadn't wanted to say anything directly because she hadn't wanted to imply anything negative about Gray. Rennie had never mentioned Gray's prison record, but that didn't mean Sarita hadn't found out some other way. She probably knew that Los and Gray had once been in a gang together. Naturally, she'd assume the worst.

Sarita couldn't possibly know that, if Los was reverting to his old ways, Gray wasn't involved.

Gray was concentrating on turning his life around. He'd explained the circumstances of his arrest, and he'd already paid for his mistake. Rennie knew he wanted to stay as far away from his former life-style as possible.

Poor Sarita. Rennie knew how long it had taken her to find someone she could be comfortable with. It would be a shame if Los turned out to be a drug dealer or a thief of some sort.

She'd have to ask Gray about this. Though Rennie didn't want to accuse Los of anything without proof, she couldn't let the matter slide for two reasons.

For one, if one of Gray's co-workers *was* involved in some kind of illegal activity, he should know about it. If something went wrong, he couldn't afford to be caught in the middle. Plus, he might be able to talk to Los and find out what was going on. He could either put Sarita's fears to rest—if Los had come by that car legitimately—or he might be able to give Los benefit from his own experience getting caught on the wrong side of the law.

Rennie felt better as she got on the interstate, heading toward her apartment. There were a lot of little details she didn't know about Gray, now that she thought about it.

For instance, what did he do all day? He didn't usually go to work at the club until late at night. At least as far as she knew.

And where did he live? Since Thanksgiving, he'd been spending most nights at her apartment. He'd never once invited her to see where he lived. When she asked him directly, he made excuses. She didn't have the phone number at his house. He'd given her his pager number. He'd said it would be easier for her to reach him that way.

Rennie didn't like the direction her thoughts were taking. She didn't know these things because they'd never come up, not because he was hiding anything from her. For the past couple of weeks, they'd been lost in their own little world. They weren't exactly doing things the way ordinary couples would.

When they were alone together, it was as if time had stopped and the outside world disappeared. This had happened often when they were teenagers. Back then they'd had a lot of good reasons for wanting to block out the real world and retreat into their own safe haven. Lately they'd fallen into that same comfortable routine. Gray would meet her after work and they would make dinner at her apartment. Then they would talk for hours. It was amazing they never ran out of things to say.

Strangely enough, though, they rarely talked about what was going on in their lives. Instead they would discuss global issues, hypothetical concepts or her favorite, whimsical fantasies that had been their staple growing up.

Sometimes Gray was so much more worldly than seemed reasonable. He would describe places he'd never been to with unbelievable authenticity. And he was so intelligent. When she asked him about his education, he told her that he spent a lot of time in the prison library during his time there. It burned her heart to know that his powerful mind wasn't being challenged to its full extent.

Yet, when she tried to focus their discussions on the future—on a career he might like to pursue or the possibility of him going back to school—Gray always changed the subject. She knew how painfully embarrassing it was for him to talk about these things with her. She never pressed it, because she didn't want to make him feel like she was looking down on him.

Especially since things had become so good between them after Thanksgiving night. Gray had a way of making Rennie feel protected and safe. She no longer had those paranoid fantasies that someone was watching her or following her. Why would anyone be interested in her boring little life, anyway?

Rennie turned off the highway exit. She was anxious to get home and see him. They had a lot to talk about tonight.

Gray drove to Rennie's house deep in thought. Today had not been a good day. He'd just left Ocean, and a few of his men were getting antsy. They were asking a lot of questions about Simon and why Gray was so hell-bent on doing business with the man.

Though Gray had thought his explanations had been sufficient, a couple of the men hadn't been satisfied. Since when were they so interested in the business side of this operation, anyway?

There had to be a reason for all the questions and suspicion he'd received from the guys lately, and he'd bet money that, once again, it all came back to TK.

The only good thing about this day was that he was going to see Rennie soon. He shouldn't invest so much of his time in her, but he couldn't help it. He would have felt guilty over the fact that he was spending so much time with her if he hadn't been afraid that she was in some kind of danger. But thankfully, things seemed to have calmed down in the past few days.

Since he still didn't know what TK was up to, he could hold on to his excuse to spend time with her. Their time together meant more to him than anything else. They were the few moments in his life that he felt completely human, like a real, living, breathing man and not some government machine, a SPEAR drone acting only on programmed commands.

In those hours he spent at Rennie's apartment, he could live as if he had free will and the choices he made were not based on his duty to his country. He could retreat into their special place where no one other than the two of them existed.

But it was also tearing him apart inside that those times when he felt most like his true self were the times he was living a lie the most. Very little of what Gray could tell Rennie was the truth. There were just too many complications and government secrets for him to be able to discuss anything in the present tense and have it be completely honest.

But he'd managed to get around that. He'd learned to steer their conversations to safe topics. Things that had nothing to do with their current surroundings or their daily lives. It hadn't been difficult; they grew up in such tumultuous times. Back then, it had been self-preservation for them not to dwell on reality. Stretching their minds to the limits of their imagination was an activity that came naturally to them.

Gray pulled over in front of Rennie's apartment building. He saw her green Volkswagen Bug in the parking lot, and he was relieved that he wouldn't have to wait for her to return home. After the day he'd had, it would feel good to lie back in her arms and forget for a while his true reason for being there.

As he got out of the car, he felt a stabbing pain in his stomach. He needed to get that checked out. He was probably getting an ulcer from all the stress in his life.

Gray didn't have the patience for the elevator, so he took the stairs, jogging up the three flights to Rennie's apartment door. He knocked three times in rapid succession. Then he waited.

He knocked again and waited. Then he

pressed his ear to the door to see if he could hear Rennie moving around inside. Nothing.

After several minutes, Gray began to worry. Quickly looking up and down the hall to make sure no one would see him, he pulled a lock-pick set out of his jacket pocket and went to work on Rennie's door.

Seconds later he pushed open the door, and his blood ran cold. All the cushions in the sofa had been overturned. The end table and lamp had been knocked over. All the drawers and cabinets in the kitchen were open. The apartment had been trashed.

Gray rushed inside, pulling out his gun. "Rennie!" He knew instantly that she wasn't there. Relief that she wasn't lying bleeding on the carpet warred with fear over her absence.

Gray gave the apartment a quick once-over trying to find any clue to what had happened. Her apartment had been broken into, and as far as he could tell, her television, VCR and stereo were missing. It seemed the intruder had grabbed the big-ticket items and split.

But a quick and dirty robbery didn't require trashing the apartment. Whoever had done this wanted to make sure it was immediately evident that the security of the apartment had been breached.

Gray's thoughts immediately went to TK. He had to be behind this. But where was Rennie? Had he kidnapped her?

He was about to tear out of the apartment, looking for one or both of them, when his pager started vibrating. It was the code Rennie used.

Gray read the number on the screen and rushed to the phone. A woman whose voice he didn't recognize answered the phone. "This is Gray. Did Rennie page me from this number?"

"Yes, hold on a second."

"Hello?"

Gray's heartbeat returned to normal at the sound of Rennie's voice. "Rennie! Where are you?"

"I'm at my friend Marlena's house. Gray, my apartment has been broken into."

"I know. I'm standing in your apartment right now."

"Inside? How did you get—never mind. Marlena called while I was making the police report."

"What did the police say?"

"Basically, they said that they've had other robbery incidents in my area recently and that they would have a patrol car drive through the neighborhood a few times tonight. I can't say that makes me feel safe."

Gray wished he could share Rennie's surprise at the cops' tepid response to her burglary, but unfortunately, he knew not to expect too much more than that.

As soon as he got off the line, *he* would make sure Rennie had someone to look after her during the times he couldn't be with her.

"Are you coming back home tonight?"

"Yes, Marlena picked me up and we were supposed to go for some coffee, but I already had the jitters, and I didn't need to add caffeine on top of them. So we just came to her place so we could talk."

"Why didn't you call me sooner? I was scared to death when I couldn't find you and I saw your apartment like this."

"I'm sorry, Gray. I was so shaken up I could barely think straight. We were just sitting here talking and I remembered that you would be coming over. I called immediately."

"Okay. Do you want me to wait here for you?"

"Yes. Marlena lives close by. I'll be there shortly."

As soon as Rennie hung up, Gray got a secure line on his cell phone and dialed Seth. SPEAR preferred that the two men spoke in person to maintain security, but Gray considered this an emergency.

Seth picked up on the first ring. "What's going on? Is something wrong?"

"I haven't got much time."

"What is it? Did Simon—"

"This isn't about Simon."

"Why not? Have you made contact yet?"

"No, not directly."

"If this isn't about Simon, then what—"

"It's Rennie. Her apartment has been broken into."

"I'm sorry—"

"I need a man put on her now. I know TK—"

"Look, Gray, I know she's important to you. I tried with the boys back at the office and they're not going to go for this. At the risk of sounding insensitive, I think the best thing you can do for Rennie is to stay away from her."

"I can't do that."

"Gray, you don't have a choice. You're about to drop the ball. Our first priority is getting Simon. Maybe if you keep your distance, the danger won't get so close to her."

"It's too late." Gray knew it was futile to argue. He'd do whatever he had to do, but he wasn't going to abandon Rennie. Especially now. "Look, don't you worry about Simon. I intend to do what I came to do."

"Good. That's what I want to hear.

Next time you call, I hope you have good news for me, buddy.''

Gray had nothing more to say, so he hung up the phone. He couldn't afford to let anyone down. If that meant he had to work double duty, he'd do it.

When Rennie walked into her apartment, Gray was leaning back on her sofa cushions, waiting for her. ''Oh, my goodness. Gray! You didn't have to clean up my apartment. I was planning to—''

He stood up and crossed the room to give her a hug. ''Shh. You've had a rough day. I didn't want you to have to come back and worry about fixing the place up. This way you can sit down and relax with me.''

He led her to the sofa, propped her feet on a throw pillow and guided her head onto another pillow resting on his lap.

She smiled, closing her eyes. ''I could get used to this.''

''Go right ahead,'' he said, massaging her temples.

After several minutes of silence as Rennie enjoyed the feel of Gray's work-roughened fingers against her temple, she shifted into a sitting position.

Curling against his side, she said, ''Gray, when are you going to invite me over to *your* apartment?''

''It's nothing special, Rainbow. Just your average bachelor pad. I'm sure you would be much more comfortable hanging out here.''

Rennie was quiet as she thought over his words. Even when they were younger, Gray hadn't liked to spend too much time at his place. But at least then, Rennie had understood the reason.

His mother had been very ill. Even though she'd tried to keep up a front for

Gray by sewing and cooking on her good days, there were always many more bad days. During those times, Gray's home had been filled with an air of sickness and grief.

Maybe his reluctance to let her see his home was rooted in old habits. If that was the case, she was sure she could ease him out of those feelings over time.

Shifting her weight to lean closer to him, Rennie tried again. "Have you ever noticed that we never spend any time out on the town? Why don't I come by the club tomorrow night—"

"No, Rennie, I don't think that's a good idea."

She sat up straight. "Why not?"

"I have to spend too much time there as it is. It's crowded and loud. It's easier to chill out here until time for me to go in to work."

"But that's what we do every night.

Don't you want to do something different?''

"We have a lot of fun here. Besides, why would I want to share you with the rest of the world when I can have you all to myself?''

They were romantic words, but Gray had been saying things like that every time she suggested they move their lives into the real world.

Usually, she accepted his excuses, mostly because she agreed. Being in each other's lives was still fresh and thrilling. She didn't mind having him all to herself. But after her conversation with Sarita, she couldn't help wondering if he was hiding something by trying to keep their relationship behind closed doors.

As soon as Rennie's thoughts went awry, she began to feel guilty. She knew Gray better than she knew herself. He may have made a few bad choices in his past, but he had a good heart. She was a trained professional. Letting her imagination run wild was wasted energy.

If she had questions, the only way to handle them was to ask whatever was on her mind directly.

As usual, Gray seemed to pick up on her pensive mood. He turned on the sofa, leaning his back against the armrest so he was facing her. "Is something on your mind, Rennie?"

She nodded. "Right as usual. I had lunch with Sarita today."

"Great. How's she doing? I haven't seen her singing at the club this week."

"She's doing just fine. We talked a lot about her relationship with Los."

Rennie wasn't sure if she saw the slight stiffening of Gray's back because she was watching him so closely or if she'd simply invented the reaction because of her curiosity.

"What did she say?"

"Well, we both agree that the work you guys do at the club takes up a lot of your time."

Gray shrugged. "Not that much." He stood. "Have you eaten?"

"I'm not hungry."

He returned a few minutes later with a sandwich and a glass of milk. "You need to go to the grocery store, Ren. You're almost out of mayonnaise."

Rennie decided to pay careful attention to how often Gray tried to change the subject. She hadn't noticed it before, but now that she was looking for it, it was clear that Gray had become adroit at dodging questions.

They never talked about daily events. He always took their conversations into the abstract.

She decided to try being more direct with her questions.

"Did you know that Los drives a BMW? Ocean must keep its bouncers very well paid."

Gray took a large bite of his sandwich, chewing slowly. At first Rennie thought he wasn't going to answer her at all.

Finally, after washing his mouthful down with a swallow of milk, he said, "It's hazard pay."

"What do you mean?"

Now she was getting somewhere. Was he going to tell her what the Ocean bouncers had to do for that kind of money?

"Ocean is a hot nightspot with very selective doormen. People are trying to crash all the time. Even the regulars can get pretty rowdy. We're paid well so we'll be willing to put up with the crap that goes with the job."

Rennie wasn't satisfied. "Yes, but isn't that extravagant?"

Gray put his sandwich down. "Rennie,

you saw the layout of the place. The front entrance alone would cost more than all four years of your college tuition. The owner is a billionaire. He can afford to be extravagant.''

Pushing his sandwich aside, Gray began nibbling on her neck.

''Enough questions. You've had a long day. What do you say we go into the bedroom and I help you relax.''

Rennie sighed as his fingers went to work on her shoulders. Okay, she was giving up. He had an answer for everything.

She hadn't asked him about Los directly, but it probably didn't matter. There was no sense in upsetting him over nothing. She hoped he didn't know anything about it.

Letting her mind relax, Rennie allowed Gray to pick her up and carry her into the bedroom.

Chapter 10

When Gray arrived at Ocean that night, he was surprised to find all his men gathered in the back room waiting for him. As he walked in, their rapid chatter came to an abrupt halt.

"What's going on?" He walked to the closet and pulled his security blazer off the hook.

Los walked to Gray and clapped him on the back. "We've all been having a little talk."

"What about?" Gray asked absently.

He was still worried about Rennie. Not only was he afraid that she was in danger, she had also been acting a bit strangely.

"We were just wondering when were going to see the mother lode you've been promising."

Everybody was so damned impatient these days.

Gray shrugged on his jacket and turned to face Los and the other men in the room. "I told you, I'm working on it."

"Are you?" Woody asked.

"What the hell is that supposed to mean?"

Los glared at Woody. "It's just that lately you haven't been around much. Me and the other guys have been moving all the shipments around here."

"I've explained all of this before. I have to set up all the connections before we can make the big score. This isn't some two-bit street deal. Orchestrating an international drug and weapons operation is a delicate business.''

''Well, then, we want to be in on setting up the deal,'' Flex said. ''Why aren't you letting us in on the negotiations?''

''Yeah,'' Woody agreed. ''We're your boys. Don't you trust us?''

''Where did you get the idea that I don't trust you?'' As soon as the words were out of Gray's mouth, he knew the answer to that question. TK. Obviously, he'd been talking to some of the guys behind Gray's back. It was no less than he'd expected.

Los quickly tried to regain control of the situation. ''It's not that we think you don't trust us. It's that we're not sure that you're concentrating on the deal as much as you could be. Maybe if you spent more time on the job, you'd get some faster results.''

It was time for Gray to get answers. ''Who have you all been talking to? I

''And?'' Gray prompted.

''And you are, boss. That's all we wanted to know.'' The other men in the room nodded and grumbled their agreement as they dispersed.

Los walked over to Gray when they were alone in the room. ''Shoot, I know how easy it is to get distracted by a woman. I messed around and let Sarita's head get pumped up. Now she thinks she owns me.''

''Yeah?'' Gray's muttered absently. All he could think about was finding TK.

''Yeah. I let her think she had control and now she keeps whining about the time I spend here at the club. What am I doing? And how come I can afford to drive a BMW? Crap like that.''

Gray's head came up, and he turned to face Los. Hadn't Rennie mentioned those same questions?

''If she doesn't stop sweating me,'' Los

continued, "I might have to put her in her place, know what I'm saying?"

Gray shrugged. "I thought you were a lover, not a fighter?" He knew that attitude hadn't originated with Los. That was the way TK thought. Apparently he'd had a bigger influence on the guys lately than Gray had realized.

Obviously that had been the plan all along. While Gray kept a close watch on Rennie because of TK's distractions, TK had the opportunity to start undermining Gray's authority. The worst part was that it had almost worked. Gray hoped he had awakened to the truth before it was too late.

"So, Los..."

"Yeah, boss?"

"When was the last time you saw TK?" When the man began to look defensive, Gray held up his hands. "It's okay, I just want to talk to him myself.

Maybe it's time we all began to work together again.''

Los's face lit up. ''That would be great, boss. Just like back in the day.''

Yeah, Gray thought. Just like back in the day, but this time *he* would call the shots.

Sarita poked her head into Rennie's office as Rennie was shutting down her computer. *''Hola, chica,* do you have a minute?''

''Sure, Sarita. You just caught me. I was on my way out.'' She walked to the sofa and sat down, patting a space next to her. ''Have a seat.''

Sarita came inside, dropped her backpack on the floor and sat on the sofa facing Rennie. ''I know you should be on your way home now. I took a chance coming so late because I didn't want to interrupt one of your sessions.''

"You can come by whenever you need to, Sarita. What's going on? Clearly it's something that couldn't wait until our group session on Friday."

"That's right. I'd rather discuss this in private. And I thought you would prefer it that way, too."

Rennie got a sinking feeling in the pit of her stomach. She knew without asking that Sarita was going to want to discuss her relationship with Los. If Sarita had found out something conclusive about Los and criminal activity, it could possible affect Gray.

Steeling herself against whatever Sarita might have to say, Rennie asked, "What's on your mind?"

"Do you remember what we talked about at the mall the other day?"

"Yes, you expressed some concern over the amount of time Los spends at the club. You were worried that he might be

involved in illegal activity. Am I right?''
There wasn't any sense in beating around
the bush.

She nodded.

''Have you discussed this with him?''

''I've tried to. Not directly, but I have
dropped some hints.''

''And what did he say?''

''He didn't take the implication well at
all. He started spouting all kinds of macho
crap about not having to answer to a
woman.''

''So he didn't confirm or deny anything.''

''Well, he sort of denied it.''

''Shouldn't that be a relief to you?''

''No, it was the *way* he denied being
involved in anything illegal. He denied before I'd had a chance to ask him anything.
Like he'd been expecting the accusation
to come up eventually, ya know? He had
a practiced answer all ready for me.''

Rennie picked up one of the throw pillows on the couch and squeezed it to her chest. Gray had given her a similar reaction when she'd questioned him. Very practiced. Gray hadn't been surprised by her questions, either.

"So the bottom line is that you don't believe the answers he gave you."

Sarita shook her head. "No. I don't. Now more than ever I'm convinced that the club is some kind of front. It would make a lot of sense based on some of the things I've seen there."

"What have you seen?" Rennie struggled to keep her voice even. She didn't want Sarita to know that Rennie's world was falling apart piece by piece right before her eyes. She'd never been in such an awkward position before. Suddenly her life had become entangled with a client's. Could she remain objective?

"Separately, the things I've seen don't

sound like much. But when you add everything up, it does get to be a bit strange. For instance, Los is a bouncer, right? But I've never actually seen him working the floor.''

''Well, it's a big club. Maybe he's just not working where you can see him.''

''Maybe, but all the other bouncers wear headsets so they can communicate. I've never seen Los with one on. Those few times I have seen him running around, he's acting more like a stock boy than a bouncer. He's usually moving a hand truck in from the loading dock or stacking crates. Or I see him huddled up talking with some other guys—who I also never see on the floor.''

Rennie forced herself not to ask if Gray was one of those men Sarita was referring to. She couldn't make this personal. She had to focus on Sarita.

"So I take it this is one of the topics you broached with Los."

"Yes. He didn't like the fact that I'd been watching him. I was supposed to sing at the club three nights this week and two nights next. I got a call this afternoon from the manager saying that they wouldn't be needing me for a while."

"You were fired?" Rennie's voice was incredulous.

"Well, the guy said he'd let me know when they needed me again, but I don't expect to hear from him again."

"And you suspect that this is Los's doing?"

"I know it's Los's doing." Sarita stared at her hands. "I don't know what to do. Everything had been going along so well. Now everything has changed."

"It's hard being in love with someone you don't trust."

The woman nodded. "The worst part is

that even knowing what I know hasn't changed my feelings for him. I still want to be with him. Does that make me crazy?''

''No, of course not. It's only natural for you to feel that way. What we want and what we need aren't always the same things. It's going to take some time for you to align your heart with your head.''

''Does that mean I have to leave him? Are you saying things are over now?''

''What do *you* think would be best?''

Sarita was quiet for a long while. ''I've worked so hard this past year to get my life on track. I don't want some man to come along and mess everything up.''

Rennie nodded, encouraging her to continue. ''But at the same time, the timing couldn't be worse. Everything is falling apart when we should be closer than ever right now.''

''What do you mean?''

Sarita looked at Rennie, clearly in conflict. There was something she wasn't saying. Just when Rennie thought she was going to confide in her, Sarita shook her head. "I don't know. I need to think about this some more. It's more complicated than you think. Maybe if I talk to him, tell him everything that I'm feeling... I don't know."

"I don't think it will hurt to talk to him and get things out in the open. Then you can decide what's best in the long haul. You don't want to undo everything you've worked for."

Sarita gave Rennie a long look. "What would you do?"

"What?" Rennie knew what Sarita was asking her but she was stalling. She could always avoid the answer by saying that Sarita couldn't frame her decisions based on Rennie, but that would be a cop-out.

They were too close for Rennie to compromise Sarita's trust with such an impersonal answer.

"What will you do if you find out there is something going on at Ocean and Gray is mixed up in it, too?"

Having Sarita rephrase the question so frankly caught Rennie off guard. For a moment, she considered her decision to be honest. Then she decided on a watered-down answer that wouldn't distract Sarita from her own issues.

"Well, if what you're saying turns out to be true, I'll have to answer the same questions myself that you're asking right now. Is the love of any man worth turning my back on what I know is right? Can I sacrifice my own hard work for another person and, if I chose to do that, how could I handle knowing I love a *man* more than I love myself?"

Sarita nodded. The two sat on the sofa

for a few minutes before Sarita excused herself and left.

Rennie continued to sit in her office thinking about what she had told Sarita. Even though she knew everything she'd said was correct, she couldn't help feeling that their situations were vastly different.

Rennie had known Gray for most of her life. She knew his soul. Yes, he'd made some bad choices in his life, but she genuinely believed he was trying to change. If she stuck by him and showed him her support...

Suddenly Rennie recognized the direction her thoughts were taking. What if she were wrong about what had been going on? Since Gray had reentered her life, nothing had been the same. In fact, things had been very strange.

First she was locked in a closet, then she had the feeling that someone was following her, and finally her apartment was broken into.

Gray had made a concerted effort to protect her lately, but maybe that was because he somehow felt responsible.

What if he was involved in some illegal activity that had managed to spill over into her life? If someone wanted to hurt him, tormenting her would be any easy task.

Rennie felt a chill slide over her heart. She didn't like having doubts about Gray. He couldn't possibly be the villain she was suddenly painting him. This was the man who sacrificed his own needs for others. Everything he'd ever done was motivated by selflessness.

Suddenly Rennie froze. What if Gray had gotten mixed up in illegal activity because he was trying to protect someone? He may have gotten caught up in a situation that was impossible for him to get himself out of.

It wasn't as though it hadn't happened before.

Rennie's heart began to hammer in her chest. She had to try to talk to him. Maybe she could get him to open up. If he had managed to get himself into trouble, that didn't mean it was too late for him to get out of it. With her help...

Rennie paused. If she were counseling someone in her situation, would she encourage the client to try to save the other person?

No, just the opposite. Was she on the verge of the kind of denial she'd seen other young women face time and again?

In her heart, she wasn't ready to give up on Gray. In her heart she still trusted him. But how many times had she instructed young women that they couldn't trust their heart's desires? After all her training, why was she suddenly so willing to ignore her own advice?

Rennie wasn't ready to answer that question yet, but she knew she had to talk to Gray. At the moment, all the answers rested with him.

Gray walked into the run-down old brick apartment building where Los had told him TK was living.

He shouldn't have been surprised by the modest surroundings, much like the places they'd all grown up. Still, TK had been famous for his big talk, and for all his maneuvering, Gray would have at least expected the man to have acquired enough to show off. Even if he still hadn't reached the big-baller status he claimed he would have by now.

Gray knocked on TK's door, half expecting not to find him at home. A few seconds later the door jerked open and TK stood before him wearing nothing but a pair of jeans and holding a forty-ounce bottle in his hand.

"G, my man," TK said with a phony grin. "What brings you to my crib?"

Gray nodded and entered the apartment behind him. "I thought it was time you and I had another little talk."

"Talk is cheap, my brother. But lucky for you that's in my price range." TK sat down on a beat-up sofa, kicked his feet up on an overturned crate serving as a coffee table and pointed Gray toward a broken recliner. "As you can see, I'm not living up to my usual standards just now."

The tone was light, but Gray could hear the animosity in TK's voice. It was as though TK somehow held him responsible for the state of his life.

"Ain't no shame in living modestly, man. It can take a while to get back on your feet after doing time in the joint."

"Didn't seem to take you long to get

rolling, did it, G? Way I hear it, you're a regular shot-caller, the big baller himself these days.''

''I made a few connections when I was in the pen.''

''And you just couldn't wait to move in on the old gang. Show them how to play with the big boys.''

Gray held his breath, hoping that if he played it cool, TK would eventually tip his hand. He seemed to have a lot of anger stored up. It was all Gray could do not to let TK know exactly how he felt about what he'd been doing to Rennie.

But Gray knew he couldn't afford to show his cards. Somehow he had to convince TK to stay away from Rennie without letting him know he knew TK was behind her recent mishaps. Even though Gray had given Los the impression that he wanted to cut TK in on their operation, he wasn't ready to do that. They were so close to Simon, and things were going to come to a head very soon.

Letting TK get involved would blow everything.

"I had to show love to my homeboys. How could I blow up and not take my boys with me?"

"Well, aren't you just the man. What's up, G? You got any love left for your boy TK?"

Gray leaned forward in the chair, locking his gaze with TK's. "What happened to the plans you told me about?"

"Things on my end aren't playing out the way I'd hoped."

"I would have loved to cut you a slice of this action, but the way I hear it, you don't have much confidence in my leadership. A few of the boys tell me that you think the money should be flowing a little faster."

"Come on now, G. Don't be getting uptight on me, man. We boys. What's a little friendly criticism?''

Gray looked around TK's apartment. ''You ran a gang for a while. Clearly you know a lot more about making loot than I do. I wouldn't want to insult you by getting you involved in an operation that may blow up in my face. What are you going to do if your deal doesn't work out?''

''TK always has a plan.''

''That's what I figured. So if your thing doesn't go as planned, you just let me know.''

TK sat silent for a few minutes, but Gray could see that his temper was boiling. It was driving him nuts that over the years their positions had become reversed.

''Tell the truth, bro. You don't know what the hell you're doing, do you? You were never hungry enough to take the real gambles. This big payoff, it ain't gonna happen. You were always all talk and no action.''

''Is that so? Well, who's got the action now? You're the only one blowing hot air around here.''

''You never had any balls. Do you think we didn't notice how you conveniently disappeared when everything was about to go down? You were always trying to talk us out of getting any action. You're not a baller. You're just a wannabe.''

Gray smiled. TK was about to crack, so he goaded him. ''Takes one to know one.''

TK released an explosive expletive, leaped out of his seat and lunged at Gray.

Gray caught him easily, taking him to the floor and pinning him there. He wanted to strangle him for the way he'd tormented Rennie, but he couldn't. For the same reason, TK hadn't come after him directly.

It surprised him how much he still believed in the code. When he'd joined the gang, he'd tried desperately to keep part of himself distanced from them. He hadn't wanted to internalize any of it. There were some things that had sunk in despite his efforts.

He'd learned loyalty and he'd learned that people didn't have to be related to be a family. And he'd learned that you didn't take down your own. No matter what.

He had to observe the code for now. He didn't have a choice. He still needed his men to respect him. But if TK did anything to hurt Rennie, the code would be meaningless.

Gray pressed TK into the floor for a second before releasing him. "Sorry there, buddy. You must have tripped." He helped a quietly seething TK to his feet.

"It was good to see you again, man. I think we're straight now, don't you? You stay out of my way, and I'll stay out of yours."

Chapter 11

Rennie stared at Gray across the dinner table while they waited for the waiter to bring the check. Dinner was over, and she hadn't broached any of the topics she'd wanted to discuss with him.

Maybe it had been the excitement of spending time together outside her apartment. For a short time, she'd been able to pretend they were a normal couple, spending a romantic evening in a restaurant together.

Yes, that was a possible explanation for

Rennie's silence, but her psychologist's mind never shut off. She knew the true reason had a lot more to do with fear than romance.

Gray leaned back in his chair, patting his stomach. "That was delicious."

"Yes," Rennie agreed absently, still caught up in her thoughts.

"What's the matter, Rainbow? You've been quiet all night. For you that's a big deal."

Here was her chance. He was giving her an opening. She tried to force herself to find the right words, or any words. "There have been a lot of things on my mind lately."

"Tough clients at the center?"

"That's part of it."

"Do you want to talk about it?"

Rennie took a deep breath. She'd never had problems expressing her feelings to Gray before. She'd known him forever.

This shouldn't be so difficult. "Yes, I think I do."

"I'm all ears. What's going on?"

Just then a high-pitched beep came from the vicinity of his belt loop. He looked down. "That's my pager. I'll be right back."

Rennie chewed on her lip while she waited for Gray. This had to be a sign. Maybe tonight wasn't the right time to get into all of this.

Then she paused, considering Gray's lifestyle. As far as she could tell, Gray only had the one job. So why did a bouncer need a pager? A club like Ocean had an army of employees. She couldn't imagine they'd have to keep the bouncers on a leash.

Rennie didn't want to send her thoughts down such a suspicious path, but once they'd started on that track, she couldn't turn them back. All the doubts and sus-

picions that had been building up were
swirling in her head. If she didn't get
some answers, she knew she'd lose her
mind.

But one thing was for certain, the restaurant wasn't private enough for the conversation she needed to have. Something
told her that she wasn't going to like the
answers she received.

A few minutes later, Gray returned to
the table. She looked up when he sat
down. "Is it an emergency? Do you have
to leave?"

"No. Everything is fine."

"Then who was it?"

"Someone from the club."

"What did he want?"

Gray gave her a puzzled look. She
didn't normally ask so many questions.
"One of the guys wanted me to take his
shift. I told him no. End of story."

Rennie nodded. He always managed to

come up with a plausible explanation. What was wrong with her? One minute she was convinced she could trust him. The next minute she was convinced she couldn't. She had to get these issues off her mind soon.

She knew he'd noticed that she had been withdrawn lately. But she had to handle this situation carefully. After spending time in prison, it would only be natural that Gray would be defensive about any accusations she might state or imply. And if she turned out to be wrong about this whole thing, she could not only damage their relationship, but his trust, as well.

After the waiter left their dinner check in front of Gray, he looked at her. "Wasn't there something you wanted to talk about?"

"Let's save it until we get back to my apartment."

"Okay, if that's what you want."

He paid the check and they exited the restaurant. They'd met there after she got off work, so they'd brought their own cars.

''Where are you parked?'' he asked.

She pointed to her lime-green Volkswagen Bug at the end of the lot.

He nodded. ''I'm parked up here. Do you want me to walk you to your car?''

She shook her head. ''No, I'll just drive up and you can follow me.''

Rennie got into her car and drove toward the highway. She started rehearsing the speech she wanted to make to Gray when they got to her apartment. She became so engrossed in her thoughts that it took her longer than it should have to notice her car was making a very peculiar noise.

She slowed down, hoping the noise would go away. After she drove a few more miles down the road, she began to smell smoke. It wasn't long before huge black clouds of smoke started spewing out of the engine.

Gray pulled up beside her, motioning for her to pull over. He parked his car behind her, then rushed over to inspect the engine.

Rennie heard him begin to curse viciously.

She dashed forward. "What's wrong? What's going on?"

He grabbed her arm and started running from the car. "The engine's on fire. We need to get out of here."

They got into Gray's car, and he threw it into reverse, backing up until they'd reached a safe distance.

Rennie watched as black smoke continued to billow out of the car. Gray dialed 911.

Before he'd finished dialing the tiny green Beetle exploded.

*   *   *

Gray entered his apartment and went straight to his bedroom. He fell facedown on his bed without removing his clothing.

What a night. After Rennie's car had blown up, they had to wait around for the fire trucks and the cops. By the time he drove her to her apartment, she had been completely wrecked.

He'd asked her if she still wanted to talk, but she had barely been able to look at him. Gray had desperately wanted to stay with her. He was certain the car had been TK's way of letting him know he hadn't appreciated the conversation they'd had. The last thing Gray wanted was to leave her alone, but she had insisted.

Rennie had told him she was too tired for company. He suggested that they just go to sleep, but she said she wanted to be by herself.

She'd been so distant and withdrawn recently, Gray knew she must have some heavy issues on her mind. It was just as well they hadn't gotten into any of those issues tonight.

If her questions had anything to do with the progression of their relationship, he wouldn't be able to give her any answers. Seth had already made it clear that it would be best if he left her alone. Of course, he could no sooner leave her alone then he could make a life with her.

He was caught between a rock and a hard place. Besides that, his entire mission seemed to be on the brink of falling to pieces.

TK was out there, lurking in the shadows, just waiting for the opportunity to move in on him. He already had Gray's men restless. They weren't sure whether or not to trust him. After all, TK had been the only leader they had known before Gray came back.

Was it all worth it? Living with constant chaos and deception? He was twenty-nine years old, and he'd never had a normal life. Chances were that before his mission was over, Rennie would have had enough of him. If everything went according to plan, he wasn't even sure if he'd stay in the country.

He couldn't ask her to wait for him. Especially when he couldn't tell her why. He'd brought enough destruction and disaster into her life. He couldn't continue to put her in danger just because she had the misfortune to be loved by him.

Gray got off the bed and headed straight for the shower. Quickly, he stripped off his clothes, welcoming the steaming hot water.

His life was a mess. He'd thought he'd been on the road to make something of his life, but what good was it all if the woman he'd done it for would never know?

He hadn't made a conscious decision to

improve his life because of Rennie, but now that he looked back on it, he couldn't help wondering. Would he ever have gotten out of the ghetto if Rennie hadn't had the guts to get out first? When she returned, she'd returned on her own terms.

Gray wished he could say the same thing. Unfortunately, the only two times he'd returned to his old neighborhood, it was under the guise of an even bigger criminal facade than when he had left.

It had never mattered before. Everyone he'd ever cared about from the old days had been long gone. Finding that Rennie had come back to set up shop had been nothing short of a complete shock. He hadn't wanted her to find him this way.

The worst part was that there was nothing he could do about his circumstances. His hands were tied. If Rennie wanted to get answers from him, there would be nothing he could offer her. No comfort and no solace. He would have to let her believe the worst about him.

Gray got out of the shower and dried himself off. He was bone tired, but a strange restlessness was working its way through his veins, making it impossible for him to sleep.

He might as well try to get some work done. If he could take care of all the details for the meeting with Simon, the operation would run smoother. The smoother things went, the sooner it would all be over.

Gray pulled out his laptop and logged onto his secured line. In a few days it wouldn't matter if his men trusted him or not. The meeting with Simon would take care of everything.

He hoped the information he'd gotten today would appease them enough to keep them in line for the next few days. The lure of more money than they'd ever dreamed of should occupy their minds for now.

Gray worked for several hours, hoping to muffle his restless thoughts. But they wouldn't be silenced.

Finally he gave up trying to outrun his thoughts and went to bed. He had to accept the reality of his situation.

Disappointments weren't new to him. This wasn't the first time he put what was best for others before his own needs. He could do it again.

Rennie sat in front of the television, staring without really seeing. She'd been that way for most of the day. For some reason, she hadn't been able to motivate herself to do much of anything.

After her car had blown up, she'd started taking public transportation to and from work. The only consolation was that the police had assured her the engine fire had been caused by some type of manufacturer's defect.

That news should have been a relief to her, but she found little comfort in it. She'd been avoiding Gray since that night. Rennie knew that wasn't the best way to handle things, but she needed some time to think things through.

She'd studied psychology and counseled hundreds of clients and suddenly she didn't know how to handle her own life. Part of her couldn't help thinking of the sweet, sensitive boy she'd grown up with. The person who would do anything for the people he cared about.

Rennie felt in her heart that she could trust him with her life. Nothing else had ever seemed so clear. But at the same time, she'd spent her entire career trying to convince her clients that it was only right to follow your heart when your head was in agreement.

If there were several logical reasons a relationship wasn't going to work, then nine chances out of ten it was better left alone.

Rennie had been rolling her own situation around in her head, and she just couldn't get around this fact. She had good reasons for being suspicious of Gray's activities, but none of them had been confirmed. And he hadn't treated her badly. Most of her clients had been treated very shabbily by their significant others.

Weren't there times when trusting in the person you loved *was* the right thing to do? Gray had hit some hard times. If she believed in him, it could only empower him to change his life. Even if he had been temporarily taken in by his old lifestyle, that didn't mean it was too late for him to change.

Rennie's doorbell rang. It was probably

Gray. She knew she wouldn't be able to put him off forever.

"I'm coming," Rennie shouted and made a run for the bathroom. She took just enough time to run a comb through her hair and change out of her pajamas into a T-shirt and jeans.

It sounded like he was leaning on the doorbell. "Just a second."

Rennie threw open the door and nearly sank to her knees.

"Oh, no, Sarita!" Rennie reached out to catch the woman before she collapsed in her arms.

Her face was bloody, bruised and tear-streaked. Sarita gripped her tightly, her body trembling.

"My God, honey, what happened to you?"

"Los beat me up." The woman's voice croaked.

Rennie closed her eyes as a wave of

sorrow washed over her. Then she shrugged it off. She had to look after Sarita before she gave in to her emotions.

"What did he do to you? You need a doctor."

Sarita shook her head. "No doctors. Please, Rennie. You're the only person I can face right now."

"Okay, sweetie, let's get you cleaned up."

Rennie helped Sarita into the bathroom where she could wash and bandage her face. As far as Rennie could tell, the extent of the damage was a black eye, a split lip, several scrapes and bruises on her cheeks and possibly a cracked rib or two.

Once she'd gotten the woman cleaned up and calmed down, they settled in the living room with mugs of hot tea. "Do you want to tell me what happened?"

Sarita nodded. "I have to tell you a lot

of things, Rennie, and you're not going to like it.''

Rennie nodded. ''I can see that.''

''No, it's worse than you think— I just don't know how to say it.''

''Then just start from the beginning. You went to talk to Los, right?''

''Yes. I thought he would be happy.'' Sarita kept shaking her head, fresh tears streaming down her face.

''Happy about what?''

''About the baby.''

''Oh, my goodness, Sarita. Are you pregnant?''

She nodded. ''I didn't tell you because I wanted Los to be the first to know. I genuinely believed he would be happy.''

''Why did he beat you up, Sarita?''

''He accused me of being a lying whore. He said the baby wasn't his.''

Rennie's temper flared. It drove her

nuts when men tried to back out of their responsibilities.

"Of course, I started yelling at him. 'Cause I ain't nobody's whore, and I told him so. He said he didn't believe me. We always used protection—but that doesn't mean anything." Sarita's tears had dried, and she was clearly angry. "I don't know what he was thinking. He knows I haven't been with anybody else."

"I don't know how much you're going to want him to be a part of your baby's life, but you can force him to take financial responsibility, Sarita."

"I guess that's what he was afraid of."

"What do you mean?"

Sarita took a deep breath, looking at Rennie sideways. "Well, this is where it begins to get really ugly."

"You can tell me anything, Sarita."

"After he got done accusing me of having someone else's baby inside me, he decided that there wasn't any baby at all. He said I was trying to trick him.''

''What? Why the hell would he think you'd do something like that?''

''I know. It's crazy, right? But it made sense to him. He started saying that this was my way of getting my hands on his share of the money.''

''What money?''

Sarita hesitated.

''You don't have to be afraid to tell me, Sarita. If he threatened you—''

''It's not just that.''

''Then what is it?''

''Rennie, the rest of this story is going to upset you.''

''Honey, everything you've told me so far is upsetting. I can handle it.''

''No, I mean it's going to upset you *personally*.''

''What do you mean?''

''It involves Gray.''

Rennie's heart started racing. She felt pricks of perspiration breaking out all over her body. She took a deep breath and said, "Sarita, if you know something about Gray, you should tell me. Especially if it's something you think I wouldn't like."

The woman exhaled a long breath. "Okay. Well, Los kept going on and on about the money. So I was like, what money? He told me not to pretend with him or he'd beat the crap out of me. That's when he hit me the first time."

Rennie flinched. "Was Gray there while Los was doing this to you?"

"No, we were alone in Los's apartment. The part about Gray has to do with the money. Los said that Gray must have told you about it, and you must have said something to me. I must have invented the baby so I would have a claim on him."

"Gray never mentioned anything to me

about money. This must be all in Los's imagination.''

''I don't think so, *chica*. He was crazed. You know, really stupid over this money, like I was really out to take it from him. He started rattling on after that. He didn't care what Gray did with his cut of the money but he wasn't going to share his with any two-bit whore.''

Rennie groaned.

''I didn't want to hear anymore,'' Sarita continued. ''I just wanted to get out of there. But before I left Los told me what they've really been doing down at the club.''

''You mean where all this mysterious money is supposed to be coming from?''

Sarita nodded.

''Are you going to tell me?''

''Are you sure you want to hear this part?''

Rennie bit her lip. ''Very sure.''

"Okay, then, here's the deal. Basically, all the guys from the old gang have been trying to get some big-time operation going for years. They could never get anything off the ground, and then their leader—I forget his name—was arrested and they all were at loose ends."

Rennie nodded. She'd known this. There had to be a lot more to the story or Sarita wouldn't be so apprehensive.

"Then Gray came back. He told them he knew how to move their operation into the big leagues. He said he'd made a lot of important contacts in prison."

Sarita paused to check Rennie's expression. Rennie motioned for her to continue. Her heart had already gone numb. She held her body stiff as she listened to what Sarita had to say.

"Los said they've been brokering weapons and distributing drugs from Ocean all along."

"Oh, my God," Rennie whispered.

Sarita nodded. "Apparently the big deal that's going to make their operation is going down soon. He said that Gray is receiving a huge shipment of weapons from some big, important dude with all kinds of international contacts. In exchange for the weapons, drugs start going out from Ocean to a worldwide cartel."

Rennie made a strangled noise. She'd known she wasn't going to like what Sarita had to say, but she hadn't been prepared for this.

Before she could begin to process what she'd learned, Sarita released a piercing scream.

"What is it? What's wrong?"

"My stomach. Los kicked me in the stomach a couple of times—" Sarita doubled over, screaming again.

"Oh, no, your baby." Rennie tried to remain calm. "We've got to get you to a hospital."

Chapter 12

"You have to go to the police," Marlena stated firmly the next day when Rennie told her what had happened.

Rennie flinched. "What? I'm sure I shouldn't even have told you. I can't go to the police." She could hardly think straight knowing Sarita was in the hospital with the life of her baby hanging in the balance.

"You don't have a choice, Rennie. This isn't petty crime we're talking here."

She folded her arms and turned away.

"I don't think I should get in the middle of this."

"It's too late now. You'd be doing the right thing."

"No, the right thing would have been staying away from Keshon Gray in the first place. Damn it, I knew better!" Hot tears began rolling down her cheeks.

"We all make mistakes, Ren. This just proves you're human like the rest of us."

"That's no excuse, Marlena. Don't you see? I do this for a living. It's my job to read people."

"Maybe, but you aren't psychic. You wanted to believe in him, so you did."

"How could I have been so stupid? I talk to women in this position every day. Women who refuse to leave their abusive husbands or boyfriends. I'm not qualified to give these people advice. I'm no better myself."

Marlena reached over and pulled Rennie close. "Now you've walked in their footsteps. This experience will make you better qualified to help your clients."

She shook her head, giving herself over to the tears.

Marlena turned Rennie to face her. "Sitting here feeling sorry for yourself isn't going to make you feel better. The only thing that will do that is time. Or even better, taking action."

"Action? The only thing I want to do right now is sleep until enough time has passed for my heart to heal."

"That's not an option. You know what I mean by action. You've got to do something about this. Don't let him get away with it."

"Stop it, Marlena. Going to the police? I just couldn't betray him like that."

"*Betray* him? Are you trying to tell me that you're worried about being loyal to a criminal? Rennie, he's the worst kind of criminal—a former gang member who's elevated himself to the lofty position of drug lord and arms dealer. And at whose expense?''

Rennie covered her ears. ''Not now, Marlena. I can't listen to this.''

''You know who he's hurting, Rennie. He's hurting the kids, and not just in L.A. If what you told me is true, he's making it possible for children all over the world to get their first taste of crack or their first weapon by the tender age of eight. You've heard the stories, and you've spoken to a lot of victims firsthand. You can't let him get away with this. This is about a lot more than just your broken heart.''

''I don't need this guilt trip right now, Marlena. Maybe in a few days, when I've had the chance to pull myself together, but I just can't deal with this now.''

''In a few days it will be too late. Isn't this deal going down in a few days?''

Rennie nodded.

"How can I get through to you?" She was quiet for a moment, then she took a deep breath. "What about Jacob, Rennie? He died the way he did because no one took the time to save him. What about all the other kids just like Jacob who don't stand a chance because someone like you won't get up off her butt and take the time to help them?"

Rennie felt like a pincushion being stabbed by a thousand tiny pins. Some pins came from Gray for all his lies and empty promises. Some pins came from her clients, whom she'd let down when she chose to follow her heart instead of doing what she knew was right. Some pins came from her friends, like Marlena, who wanted to save her from herself.

But most of the pins came from her own conscience. She couldn't betray herself again. This time she'd tell her heart to go to hell and do what her head knew was right. She'd do what Jacob would want her to do. Nothing could save Gray now. Her only choice was to try to stop him from hurting others.

"All right," she said quietly. So quietly that Marlena was still ranting about her duty as a human being and didn't hear her. "I said all right."

"And if you don't, I will—what?"

"You win. I'll talk to the police."

Marlena gave Rennie a quick hug. "I promise you won't regret this."

"Well, the advice you're giving me now is the same advice I've given my clients. It's about time I started taking some of that advice for myself."

"Don't worry about a thing. I'll take care of the details. I have some friends down at the LAPD. I'll make sure they make this as easy on you as possible. No paperwork, no exhaustive questioning sessions. You'll just walk in, tell them what you know and walk out. Simple.''

Simple wasn't the word for what Rennie went through that afternoon. Apparently, the LAPD was starved for a hot tip like this. They wanted the weapons Gray was bringing in and they expected Rennie to help them get what they needed.

Suddenly her voluntary confession came with mandatory participation. They wanted to wire her bedroom and get her to extract enough information out of Gray to ambush him.

Rennie didn't understand why she couldn't hate Gray. She hated what he planned to do. She hated that he'd lied to her. But she couldn't hate the man himself.

The things Sarita had said about him didn't fit the man she'd fallen in love with. She hadn't let go completely. Part of her was still hoping that this was all some giant mistake. She'd allowed Marlena to convince her to speak with the police, but buried underneath the pain and shattered dreams, there was still a tiny granule of hope.

Until she heard the confession from his own lips, that hope would live on. She felt pathetic and desperate for clinging to hope, but she couldn't help herself. There was still the slimmest of chances that Gray wasn't involved in whatever was going on at the club. Maybe he'd just gotten caught in the middle. Maybe Los had used Gray's name because he didn't want to put his own neck on the line.

Rennie could come up with excuses all day for not believing that Gray had betrayed her. But those were for her fantasy world. Unfortunately, Rennie was all too aware that she lived in the real world.

And in the real world, she had to face the fact that Gray was indeed a criminal.

That evening the police arrived disguised as carpet cleaners so they could bug her apartment.

Rennie didn't want to stick around, so she went to the hospital to see Sarita.

"Hey, *chica,* are you feeling any better today?"

Sarita turned to face Rennie. One eye was turning purple, and her lower lip was divided by a thick red scab. Sarita's normal brilliance—her red hair, her fiery dark eyes and golden skin—all seemed pale and dull against the sterile white hospital background.

She pulled herself into an upright position when she saw Rennie in the doorway. Her eyes were welling with tears. "I lost the baby, Rennie."

"Oh, Sarita." Rennie rushed to her side

to give her a comforting hug. As if the poor woman hadn't been through enough in her life. It wasn't fair that she had to suffer this way.

The woman stared at her hands. "It's probably for the best, right? What kind of mother would I have been? I can't even take care of myself. How could I have taken care of a child?"

"You would have been a wonderful mother, Sarita. You know I wouldn't say it if it weren't true."

Rennie couldn't help feeling responsible for the way things had turned out. She felt as though she hadn't just failed herself, she'd failed Sarita, as well.

There must have been signs. Why hadn't she been able to give the young woman some warning before things had gotten to this level? She knew about Los's past. She should have said something.

Instead, she'd listened to Gray. She

hadn't wanted to get in the way of someone who was trying to move on with his
life. If they had all been shooting for a
more positive lifestyle, as he'd told her,
the last thing any of them needed was
Rennie looking down her nose at them.

She should have trusted her instincts.
Those men were bad news when she'd
first met them, and nothing had changed.

Sarita was quiet, trying to pull herself
together. "You just missed my sister, Is-
abelle. I wanted you to meet her."

"I would have come sooner, but I had
to go to the police station. I told them
what I know."

"*Aiy Dios,* Rennie. Los will kill me if
he finds out that I told you."

"Don't worry, I never mentioned your
name. I only told them about Gray. Sarita,
this is all my fault. I trusted the wrong
man, too. This should show you that even

with years of training, psychologists screw up their personal lives, too.''

"So what do we do now? We're two women scorned. How do we put our lives back together?''

Rennie didn't feel qualified to give advice at that moment. "You don't want my advice right now, Sarita.''

"Why not? Because you're human, too? Rennie, you've not only been my shrink, you've been my friend. Talking to you has gotten me through some tough times. I hope you don't think you can abandon me now that I need you most.''

Rennie felt tears filling her eyes. She wasn't sure what to say. Sarita, who seemed to understand what she was feeling, simply held her arms open. Rennie leaned down and gave her a firm hug.

Sniffling, she pulled back. "Now let's see, what do we do next? Well, for you the answer is clear. The first step is to get yourself healthy again. Then you're going to finish nursing school and go back to work at the hospital. This setback doesn't have to derail everything you've been working for."

Sarita nodded. "So what about you, Rennie? Are you going to do the same thing?"

"I don't have a choice. I have a few more details to iron out in this mess, and then I have to try and put this all behind me."

Gray let himself into Rennie's apartment, his mind heavy. Everything was falling apart on him. He'd just left the club, and the guys were starting to slack off. Los had been nowhere to be found, leaving Flex to load the trucks by himself.

Thank goodness this whole mess was nearly over. He'd spoken with Simon's right-hand man that morning. Next time he would deal with Simon directly. That bastard was so close Gray could smell him. He just had to hold everything together for a few more days.

Gray was surprised not to find Rennie in the living room waiting for him. He was worried about her. She'd been avoiding him for the past few days, and she'd sounded so strange when she'd called to make sure he was coming over to see her tonight.

Her apartment was dark. "Rennie!" he called, praying nothing was wrong.

"In here." Her voice came from the bedroom.

He paused in the doorway and found her lying on her bed. "What's wrong, honey?"

She sat up. "I had a headache so I came in to lie down for a few minutes."

He moved forward to sit on the edge of her bed, reaching out to feel her forehead.

"You're not coming down with something, are you?"

She pulled away from his hand, curling up on the other side of the bed. "I don't think so. I took some aspirin. I'm sure I'll be fine soon."

"Did you eat? Do you want me to make you something?"

"No."

He stood, heading for the closet. "You're shivering. Let me get you another blanket."

"Stop fussing over me," she snapped.

Gray whipped around. "Honey, what's wrong?" He move to the edge of the bed and sat.

Rennie stared at her hands. "I just came from visiting Sarita in the hospital."

"Oh, my God, what happened? Is she all right?"

Rennie snorted. "Are you trying to pretend that you don't know?"

Gray shook his head in confusion. "Should I know?"

"Los beat her up."

"I'll kill him," he muttered under his breath. Suddenly, Rennie's odd behavior was beginning to make sense. "I'm so sorry, Rennie. I really had no idea. Believe me, I'll take this up with him. How is Sarita doing?"

"She went to tell him she was pregnant, and he beat the crap out of her. He wouldn't even admit that the baby was his. After he gave her a black eye and some broken ribs, he walked out on her. She came straight to my apartment. While we were talking, she started having stomach pains, and I had to rush her to the hospital. She lost the baby."

Gray shook his head. "Poor kid, she didn't deserve that."

"No, she didn't, but I don't want to talk

to you about Sarita and Los. I want to talk to you about us.''

''What about us?''

''You've been lying to me.''

Gray's throat tightened. He gripped the edge of the bed. She didn't know the whole story, so that meant Los must have let something slip to Sarita. Sarita must have passed it on to Rennie. He couldn't have asked for lousier timing. He'd been waiting for the other shoe to drop for weeks, and he'd finally managed to convince himself it might not happen.

He had to admit that part of him had hoped he would be able to keep Rennie in the dark long enough to complete his assignment. Then there was a chance he could ditch his cover once and for all and tell Rennie the truth.

He hated lying to her. It became harder and harder the more time he spent with her. He'd give anything not to have to lie to her anymore.

"What do you mean?" he said, stalling for time. It was better to let her tell him whatever it was she thought she knew.

"I mean you've been lying to me about everything. You told me that you wanted to put your life back together, that you were trying to change."

"Yes, I did tell you that."

"And it's not true, is it?"

"That depends on how you look at it."

"Oh, will you just stop it? Stop being vague and trying to pretend you don't know what I'm talking about."

"All I know is that you think I've been lying to you. But I know I've been honest about the only things that matter. I never lied when I told you that I love you. And I never lied about what we have together."

"None of those things matter now."

"Why not?"

"Because you're not the man I thought you were. I don't know who you are anymore. Tell me the truth. Please. If you ever loved me, tell me the truth."

"About what exactly?"

"About what you've been doing at the club."

Gray tried not to flinch. He'd known it was coming, but part of him had hoped she was going to say something he could easily talk his way out of. Maybe he could answer her questions without lying this time. If she could just hold on a little while longer, everything would be over.

"It's true that things aren't what they seem, but I need you to trust me right now, Rennie."

"How can I trust you when I know that you're breaking the law?"

Gray released a heavy sigh. "Sometimes you need to work on the opposite side of the law to do what needs to be done."

"And what exactly is it that needs to be done?"

"It's better for you not to know the details, Rennie. That way no one can accuse you of aiding and abetting."

"I don't care about that right now. I just want you to tell me the truth."

Why didn't she just ask for a pint of his blood? That would be easier to deliver. "I know you're upset about Sarita, Rennie, but that wasn't my doing. Los will answer to me for hurting her. Whatever she told you—"

"She told me that you and the other guys are trading drugs and guns out of the club. Is it true?"

Gray rested his forehead in his hands. There was no easy way to break a woman's heart.

"You don't really want to know the answer to that question, do you?"

Rennie clutched her pillow to her chest, rocking back and forth. Tears rolled silently down her face. Gray had hoped to never see the look in Rennie's eyes he saw at this moment.

"Sweetheart, please—"

"Go on, tell me the rest."

He shook his head. "Don't torture yourself like this, Rennie. Someday I'll be able to explain all of this to you."

"Don't bother, I'll never understand how you could let me down this way."

"I don't know what else to say to you."

"Sarita said there's a big deal that's about to go down. Is it taking place at the club?"

"Rennie, I can't—"

"I'm only asking because my friends still hang out there. Alise's birthday is in a few days and she has mentioned going to Ocean. I don't want them walking into the middle of something.''

''There shouldn't be any activity until early in the morning, after the club is closed. But just to be safe, tell them to stay away from there for the next few days.''

''How many days?''

''Three.''

Rennie's eyes filled with tears, and she flopped back against her pillows. ''I have nothing more to say to you, Gray.''

''Then just listen. I know you think you understand everything right now, but you don't. What goes on out there—'' he pointed to her bedroom window ''—doesn't change what I feel for you.''

A strangled noise erupted from her throat.

''I know you don't believe that. I don't expect you to right now. But I promise you, Rainbow, one day this will all make sense.''

Rennie rolled onto her side, her back to him. He could tell she was still crying. ''Please, I just want you to leave now.''

Gray nodded, then trudged to the door. Nothing in his life had ever been this painful.

Gray left Rennie's apartment feeling sick to his stomach. It wasn't just the pain of having to hurt Rennie the way he had. There was something else.

He drove home slowly trying to remember why he'd joined SPEAR, trying to decide if the years he'd given away had been worth it. If he hadn't joined SPEAR and traveled the world, living someone else's life, would he and Rennie have had a chance at a life together?

He wanted the answer to be yes, but deep down inside he knew it wasn't.

SPEAR had given him a direction when he'd had none. If he'd stayed in L.A., Rennie might have come back to discover the horrible things she believed about him now were true.

Hurting Rennie was the last thing he wanted to do, but he had to take comfort in the fact that he was doing the right thing. Once they had Simon in custody, the world would be a better place. He'd done a lot of good during his time with SPEAR. No matter how much he wanted to blame SPEAR for his lack of a personal life, it was because of the agency that he could sleep at night.

He knew there were fewer terrorists in action because of SPEAR. He knew there were thousands of men, women and children whose lives had been saved thanks to SPEAR agents. A portion of those lives he'd rescued personally.

Gray's doubts began to resurface. It was

his mission. Had he told her too much? He hadn't wanted to put her in the middle of the bust, so he'd tried to tell her just enough to keep her out of the way.

Following his instinct, Gray paged Seth. Within minutes his telephone rang.

"What's up, partner?"

"Seth, I've got a strange request, but I need you to trust me on this."

"Anything. What is it?"

"We need to postpone the bust."

"Anything but that."

"Okay, then let's change the location or the time."

"Why? What's happened?"

"Everything is falling apart. Things at the club are in chaos."

"You made contact with Simon's man, didn't you?"

"Yes, you know I did."

"And everything's in place, right?

Simon's going to be there in person.
That's all we need.''

"Look, Seth, it's more complicated
than that. I've just got this feeling that if
we try to rush this, we'll regret it. I think
TK is going to try to make a move. All
I'm asking for is a few extra days to make
sure everything goes off as planned.''

"I understand where you're coming
from, Gray, but my hands are tied on this
one. Jonah's pushing us to wrap this up as
soon as possible.''

"You won't even pass my request
along?''

"I could do that, but we both know it's
going to be denied. Let's not waste any
more time. Hang in there. The end is
near.''

Gray hung up the phone unable to shake
the sick feeling. They wouldn't hold off
the mission so much as a day. He didn't

know why he felt so adamantly about this, but he did.

All he could do was cross his fingers and hope that thing went according to the plan.

TK sat in Ocean's VIP lounge sipping Dom Perignon. It hadn't taken him long to become accustomed to the expensive champagne. It wouldn't be long before he'd have the houses, cars and women that went with it.

Gray wasn't working at Ocean tonight. TK smiled. This was the way he liked it, with Gray out of the picture. It was time to remove him permanently.

Thanks to TK, there was trouble in paradise. Gray's lady love may not want anything to do with him anymore, but that didn't mean that Gray wouldn't do whatever it took to save her.

No more games. Los had already told

him everything he needed to know. Soon, all his old gang would be working for him again. Everything would be as it should have been from the start. Money rolling in, a phat club to chill in and all his boys doing what he told them to do.

Gray wouldn't be able to get a job driving a cab in L.A. He'd see to that. He couldn't take Gray down the regular way, but that was okay. This way was a lot more painful.

He liked watching Gray suffer as he stripped him of everything he'd worked for, piece by piece.

And he was going to start with that beautiful girlfriend of his. He was getting bored with toying with her, anyway. It was time to get to the grand finale.

Chapter 13

Why did doing the right thing feel so much worse than doing the wrong thing?

Rennie had been pacing her apartment for most of the morning. She couldn't get last night's scene out of her head. It had crushed her to watch everything she'd had with Gray go up in flames.

She hated herself for wanting to forget the whole mess and trust him the way he'd asked her to. Thank goodness she knew Officer Novato had been listening to every word. It had forced her to be strong.

Rennie had always believed she was a strong woman. It killed her to know she'd allowed herself to be turned away from everything she believed in for a man. Yes, she could better identify with her clients, and she was sure that empathy would help her counsel women in the future. But it didn't help her like herself right now.

Even more, she blamed Gray. He knew she'd never be able to live with his crimes. If he'd been any kind of man, he would have stayed away from her. It wasn't fair for him to have put her in this position.

Rennie dredged her mind for all the excuses to hate Gray she could find, and in the end, they weren't enough. She still loved him, and she'd have to deal with that for the rest of her life.

Rennie pressed her fingers to her temples. She *knew* she'd done the right thing, yet turning the man she loved over to the police was tearing her apart. Life had been difficult for Gray. She'd just guaranteed that it would get harder.

Unable to remain cooped up in her apartment, she decided to go for a walk. The streets were cluttered with Christmas shoppers hurrying from one store to the next. Rennie felt deeply sad, and she knew it showed on her face, but no one noticed as they rushed around her.

In some ways, her invisibility was a relief, and in others it was another pinprick in her heart. She didn't want to speak to anyone or explain the source of her heartbreak, but it hurt that no one cared. For all the pain welling inside her, it should matter to someone other than herself.

But her pain made no impact on the world. She wasn't the first person to have her heart broken, and she wasn't the first woman to discover her lover lived a double life. All the signs had been there, and she'd chosen to ignore them.

Sinking onto a park bench, Rennie pulled her jacket closed around her neck. She sighed loudly, letting her head fall back against the slatted wood.

"Do you mind if I sit down?"

Rennie's head jerked up. An attractive man with a congenial smile was motioning to the empty space beside her.

Feeling a hot flush rush up her neck, she nodded.

"No, don't go," he said, when she started to get up. "I was looking to take a break from all the Christmas madness. Have you finished your shopping yet?"

She chewed her lip. "I haven't even started. I've had a lot on my mind lately."

"I can see that. Why don't you unload a few things here. It will probably make the trip home a lot lighter."

Rennie laughed. The man looked a few years older than she was. Good-looking, friendly—and he was clearly hitting on her. It was a bit of a relief to see that life wasn't over after a failed relationship. No matter how big a disaster her life was now, at least she knew she was still attractive to men—once she could trust them and herself enough to try again.

"That's very nice of you to offer to listen. But I listen to other people's problems for a living, and I'm just not that good at sharing with a stranger myself."

"Ah, so you're either a shrink or a bartender."

She laughed. "The first one."

"Well, have you ever tried unloading your problems on a stranger? The same rules apply to park benches that apply to bars. Whatever you say doesn't leave here."

"My story's really not that unique. Basically, I discovered that the man I'm in love with isn't who I thought he was."

"Ooh," the man said, pretending to

stab himself in the chest. "It may not be unique but that doesn't make it any less painful, does it?"

"No, it doesn't. And there's nothing I can do to make the pain go away."

"Maybe I can help."

"Thanks for the offer, but I don't think so."

He laughed. "Don't worry, I'm not making a move on you...yet. I just thought we could go get a cup of coffee." He rubbed his hands together. "Somewhere a little warmer."

Rennie stood. "It was really nice talking to you, but I think I'm just going to head back home."

The man stood, too, and turned to face her. Something about him was very familiar. The more she studied his face, the more she was certain she knew him.

Before she could ask him about it, his

face broke into a wide grin. His gaze dropped to his pocket.

Rennie saw a flash of metal and followed his gaze. He'd pulled the butt of a gun out just far enough for her to tell what it was.

''Are you sure you don't want to reconsider that coffee?''

Gray stared at the floor plan of Ocean until his vision blurred. The location of each SPEAR agent on the scene had been carefully diagrammed. Each step from the word hello to the final arrests had been choreographed to the last detail.

Simon was going down tonight.

Seth had taken care of everything. Logically, Gray knew his partner was right. The operation was under control, and the mission should go off without a hitch.

But, in his heart, something didn't feel quite right.

Standing, Gray stretched and moved away from his desk. He prowled around the room, trying to free the nervous energy coiling in his stomach.

He paused by the night table, his eyes captured by a photo lying next to his alarm clock. He picked it up, and a smile curved his mouth.

Rennie had taken the picture, the last shot on her roll of film. She'd set the camera on the end of her coffee table, then had rushed to the couch to get into the shot. They'd wrapped their arms around each other and huddled low on the sofa to fit into the frame.

The result was an adorable picture of the two of them cuddling like koala bears with silly grins on their faces.

Gray ran his fingers over Rennie's face. A hard knot formed in his stomach. The picture slipped out of his fingers.

He groaned, clutching his gut. This

wasn't an ulcer. After his last bout of pain, he'd gotten a full examination. His doctor, part of the SPEAR organization, had signed him off in perfect physical health.

Sinking onto the edge of his bed, Gray inhaled several deep breaths until the pain eased to a mild spasm. He began to think over to the past few weeks.

The last time he'd felt his stomach cramping had been seconds before Rennie's car had blown up. The time before that, her apartment had been burglarized. Before that, she'd been locked in a closet. He swallowed hard, feeling his heart thundering in his chest.

This wasn't the first time he'd had a physical reaction to danger. A not-quite-painful tension in the muscles of his gut had saved his life more than once. In the field, there wasn't time for analyzing. He had to act on instinct.

Gray knew he didn't have any psychic

abilities, but it wasn't much of a stretch for him to believe that Rennie's soul was connected to his.

Even when they had been teenagers, they'd completed each other's thoughts and had communicated feelings without using words. When she was happy, he felt it like warm sunshine on his skin. When she was sad, it was like clouds passing over the sun, leaving him in cold shadows.

Right now, he knew something was wrong with Rennie. It didn't matter how he knew it. All that mattered was getting to her before it was too late.

Rennie glared at TK's profile as he slouched in the motel recliner, laughing at a sitcom rerun on cable. If she'd realized who he was a few minutes faster, she might have been able to get away from him before he'd pulled that gun on her.

She shifted on the bed, trying to find a

position that didn't strain her arm, which was handcuffed to the slatted headboard.

TK turned, pointing his gun at her. "Be still over there."

"My arm is falling asleep."

He lowered the gun. "Quit complaining. I gave you the bed, didn't I? Or is it that you're getting lonely? Want me to come over there and join you?"

Rennie choked down her fear. So far, her only comfort had been that raping her didn't appear to be a part of his plan. "Don't you dare."

TK laughed, putting the gun on the table beside him. "Don't sound so offended, sweetheart. I'm the only company you're going to have for a while. You'd better learn to enjoy it."

"There will be people looking for me soon."

"What people? You don't mean G, do you? From what I've seen, the two of you aren't exactly on speaking terms right now.''

''Have you been watching me?''

He ignored her question. ''Even if for some reason he did come looking for you, he wouldn't find you here. Sometimes the best hiding places are right under a brother's nose.''

''What do you mean?''

TK laughed again, clearly impressed with his cleverness. ''This motel is practically across the street from his apartment. He'd run all over town before he thought to check here.''

Rennie sighed heavily. ''There's no ransom on the line. If you don't expect Gray to come after me, why am I here?''

TK picked up his gun and walked to the bed. He studied her for a long moment, causing her to curl into a ball at the opposite edge of the bed. He ran the nose of the gun along the line of her jaw. "Don't underestimate your value, sweetheart."

Rennie turned her head, trying to move as far away from him as possible. So far, he'd refused to give her a straight answer about his plans. She knew he needed her alive for now, but Rennie had no idea when her luck would run out.

Sarita had told her TK was trying to find a way to encroach on the operation. Rennie thought she was protecting Gray by going to the police. TK was supposed to step into the middle of everything and be arrested with the others.

Now things weren't going to be that simple.

"Does this have something to do with the weapons deal going down tonight?" Maybe if she baited him enough, she could find out what he was up to.

TK's brows raised in amusement.

''Well, now, what do you know about that?''

''I know when and where. Is that what you want to know?''

''Aren't you a helpful sister?'' He sat in the recliner, watching her. ''Thanks, but I already have all the information I need. Lay back. Relax. We're going to be getting up real early in the morning.''

Rennie stiffened as a wave of nausea washed over her. That had to mean he was going to the club, and he planned to take her with him.

It took Gray thirty seconds to pick the lock on Rennie's apartment door.

He'd telephoned several times on his way over, though he suspected she was probably screening her calls.

Her rental car was parked in her reserved space, but she didn't answer the doorbell. Even if she'd been adamantly avoiding him, she would have come to the door after he began pounding on it and calling her—if for no other reason than to keep him from disturbing her neighbors.

Two tenants poked their heads out to find out what he was up to. Gray had been forced to leave for several minutes. Then he returned to pick the lock.

Once inside, Gray called her name, then looked through each room. She wasn't there.

Wherever she'd gone, Rennie clearly hadn't been planning to be gone long. She'd left her stereo playing in the living room, and there was a bag of movie rentals sitting in front of the television set. It looked like she had been planning a quiet Friday evening at home.

He checked out the kitchen and found a package of pork chops thawing in the sink. Ever since she'd successfully prepared Thanksgiving dinner for the two of them, Rennie had taken an interest in cooking. She'd started collecting recipes from friends and co-workers, and would call him up in the afternoon to tell him what new dish she planned to try out on him that night.

Gray knew there wouldn't be any more lunchtime phone calls or dinners prepared side by side in her tiny kitchen. He could accept that she was no longer be a part of his life—as long as he knew she was safe.

Unfortunately, the knot in his gut told him differently.

Searching through her desk, Gray found her address book. He picked up the phone and started dialing.

"Hello?"

"Marlena, this is Gray."

"I have caller ID. What the hell are you doing calling from Rennie's apartment?"

"Have you seen her? I'm afraid she might be in trouble."

"As long as you're in her apartment, she is. What did you do, break in? If you don't get out of there right now, I'm calling the police."

"Good. When you do, tell them Rennie is missing."

The woman paused for a long moment. "Missing? How could Rennie be missing? I'm sure if you can't find her it's because she just doesn't want to see you."

"I understand that, but I need to make sure that she's all right. Just keep an eye out for her, okay?"

The urgency of his tone must have finally gotten through to Marlena. "What do you think could have happened to her?" she asked softly.

"I'm not sure, but you have to trust me on this. She could be in danger. If you do find her, don't let her out of your sight."

"Okay."

Gray hung up the phone and dialed again.

"Alise, have you seen Rennie?"

"Who is this?"

"It's Gray."

"Please leave her alone. This is hard enough on her as it is."

"I don't want to bother her. I just want to make sure everything is okay. Do you know where she is?"

"No, but even if I did, I wouldn't tell you. She doesn't want to be with you anymore."

"I understand that, but I think she's missing."

"No, I'm sure she just went out for the evening. It's Friday night."

"I don't think so. Her rental car's out front and she left her stereo on."

"Are you inside her apartment?"

"Look, I'm not asking you to contact

me if you find her, just make sure she's all right. Can you do that?''

''Of course, I'll do whatever Rennie needs.''

He hung up and called several other numbers. He got the same frosty reception from most of her friends and co-workers, but everyone agreed to watch out for her.

After leaving Rennie's apartment, Gray checked all the stores and public areas within walking distance. Sometimes, when she had a lot on her mind, she liked to walk it off. She said it helped her clear her head. He checked her office, her favorite coffee shop, the bookstore and all her other favorite spots.

On a hunch, he decided to check out TK's apartment. He didn't see his car out front. After a few knocks for good measure, he picked the lock.

What he saw made his heart freeze.

The place had been cleaned out. No furniture, no clothes in the closet, no food in the refrigerator. Nothing. The man hadn't left so much as a dust bunny behind.

It was too much to hope that TK had left town, but finding out exactly where the man was shouldn't prove too difficult.

Gray pulled out his cell phone and paged Seth. His phone rang minutes later.

"What can I do for you, Gray?"

"I want you to contact the guy you have tailing TK. I want to know exactly where he is. I'm standing in his apartment right now, and the place has been cleared out."

"Uh, that may be a bit of a problem."

The fist clenching in his abdomen tightened. "What do you mean?"

"I hate to tell you this, Gray, but TK shook off our man in East L.A. early this morning. We don't know where he is."

Gray spat out a violent curse. "Rennie's missing and you're telling me we have no idea where TK is.''

''Don't worry, we're on top of it. I'm sure one of our men will pick him up again before tonight.''

''That's not good enough. He's got Rennie.''

''You don't know that.''

''I'll tell you what I know. The mission is screwed. We can't go through with it.''

''We haven't got a choice. Simon is so close we can smell him. We can't let him slip through our fingers this time. If we cancel at the last minute, we may never get another shot at him.''

''That's a risk we're going to have to take.''

''Sorry, Gray, but my orders come straight from Jonah. Don't worry about TK and Rennie. Let us handle them. You just concentrate on collecting that weapons shipment and nailing Simon. Do you hear me? SPEAR is your first and only priority right now.''

''I'll do what I have to, but don't say I didn't warn you.''

Rennie lay still, trying to make sense of her situation while TK watched television. Finally, she couldn't take it any longer.

''Is that all you're going to do tonight?''

He turned, his mouth full of microwave popcorn. ''What? You got something against the WB network?''

''No, but don't you have to prepare or something? You're going to Ocean to crash the party, aren't you?''

''That's right. G's not coming to us because we're going to him.''

''What could you possibly stand to gain from taking me along? You said yourself that Gray and I aren't a couple anymore.''

''Just because he's ain't knocking your

boots doesn't mean he's going to stand around and let me kill you. In fact, I think he'd do just about anything to prevent that.''

"So you want…what? Money? You want him to hand over whatever he's getting from this big transaction?''

"Oh, no, this is more than just a one-shot deal. I want it all. I want him out of the picture for good.''

"I don't get it. If that's all you wanted, why didn't you just shoot him?''

TK's laugh was harsh. "You never did get it, did you? That's why you started tripping when little J went down. You never understood what it meant to be in a gang.''

"What does my brother have to do with this?''

"Everything. Little J had heart. He wasn't real hard, but he was loyal. Down till the end.''

Rennie jerked the chain on her handcuffs, wishing to be free just long enough to smack that smug grin off his face.

"Now, your man G was different. He never had the heart. Sure, he was plenty hard, but he thought he was too smart for the rest of us."

"He was and still is." The words were automatic, but Rennie instantly regretted them.

TK shot to his feet and got in her face, close enough for her to feel his breath on her chin. His black irises glittered with hatred as they narrowed into slits.

"He's not as smart as he thinks, little girl." TK spat the words.

Rennie drew back, afraid he might strike her, but it seemed TK was in a world of his own.

"I'm going to have it all this time. Me." He pounded his chest savagely.

"I'm going to have back what he stole from me."

Trembling, Rennie watched as TK paced the room, muttering to himself. He faced her, waving his gun.

"Don't expect your boyfriend to save you this time. He's been playing out his league for a while now. I'm the big baller around here. He should have been working for me. G didn't want to cooperate, so now he gets nothing."

All Rennie could do was stare in amazement at the maniacal gleam in his eyes.

"Tonight he's going to watch me take it all. His money. His friends. And after he watches me put a bullet through your head, he'll beg me to take his life."

Chapter 14

At three-thirty in the morning, Gray stood on the nightclub roof staring out over the City of Angels. Simon was scheduled to arrive in an hour, and Gray still didn't know what had happened to Rennie.

"Gray." A woman's voice called him.

"Rennie?" He spun around to have his worst fears confirmed. TK stood behind her with a gun to her head.

"Hey, G. You forgot to invite us to the party, so we decided to crash."

Gray swallowed hard. He had to remain

calm so Rennie wouldn't be hurt. "Let her go, TK. This is between you and me."

TK laughed. His cocky spirit had returned. "Let her go? That wouldn't be any fun."

"What's the matter? You knew you couldn't take me on by yourself, so you have to hide behind a woman? You always loved to imply that I couldn't handle myself, but it looks to me like you're the coward."

Gray prayed he could keep the battle verbal for a while. The place was crawling with SPEAR agents. They were already in position. When he failed to show up downstairs, someone would come find him.

"You can't clown me now, G. I'm running this show. I know you're strapped. Take your gun out nice and slow and put it down."

Gray did as he was told. He couldn't

take any chances with Rennie's life. TK had an arm locked around her waist, pinning her to his side. She stared at Gray with wide eyes that pleaded for him to do something.

Their eyes met. Gray promised himself, as soon as he got the opportunity, he would make sure TK paid for making Rennie suffer.

"That's better. Now, I have an appointment downstairs, and I don't want to be late. It's a shame you won't be able to make it, G."

TK pulled the gun away from Rennie's head and cocked it. Rennie must have assumed TK was about to fire on Gray.

"No," she shouted, hurling her body at TK and knocking the gun from his grasp.

"Why, you little—" TK whirled on Rennie, clearly intending to strike her, but Gray had no intention of letting that happen.

He grabbed TK by the shoulders. TK whirled, focusing all his rage at Gray in one powerful blow.

Gray staggered backward but caught himself quickly. Hunching over, he rushed forward, ramming TK in the stomach with his head.

TK went down, and Gray followed him. He pulled TK to his feet and hurled him at the brick wall beside the door to the stairs.

Gray turned to check on Rennie. He found her huddled behind a power generator. "Rennie, are you okay?"

She peeked out and opened her mouth to answer him. "Gray, look out."

TK flew at Gray's back and brought him to the ground. They rolled across the cement, exchanging punches.

Gray was the more skilled fighter, combining several martial arts with down-and-dirty street fighting, but TK had the power of pure malice on his side.

The man had nothing left to lose. He was fighting with everything he had. No matter how many times Gray delivered a slug that should have kept TK down for the count, TK wouldn't give up.

He could hear Rennie screaming in the background. Gray wasn't going to give up easily, either. There was too much at stake. Despite the pain, he kept fighting.

If he lost this battle, there was no telling what would happen to Rennie. The danger she faced was because of him, and he had to make sure she came out of this alive. He owed her at least that much.

TK buried his fist deep in Gray's gut, and Gray could feel the salty taste of blood on his lips. He lay on the concrete while TK pounded on him, cussing him out with the fervor of a madman.

Gray gathered his strength and bucked

TK off him. He pressed his advantage, dragging both of them to their feet.

Gripping TK by the throat, Gray drove the man backward into the brick wall.

Taking advantage of TK's dazed state, he gripped his neck in a wrestling hold and applied constant pressure until TK lost consciousness.

Gray let go, and TK collapsed in a heap at his feet.

"Is he dead?"

Gray looked up to find Rennie standing over him. "No, he's just…unconscious."

"That thing that you just did…how—"

He shook his head, not sure how to answer her. "Are you okay? Did he hurt you?"

Rennie wrapped her arms around her body, shivering from the cold night air. "I'm—I'm…"

Gray couldn't bear to watch the violent shakes racking her body. He pulled her into his arms and held her tightly, half expecting some resistance.

But she didn't try to fight him. Instead she seemed to sink into his embrace gratefully, clutching him as she burrowed her face into his chest.

They held each other for several minutes, and for that short time, Gray allowed himself to pretend that he had the right to hold her. He hadn't been sure that she would ever permit him to touch her again.

"Sweetheart, I'm so sorry about this," he said, pulling back. "When I realized you were missing, I nearly lost my mind."

"How did you know?"

Gray stroked the back of her head. "I just knew."

"Are you still planning to, um, do business tonight?"

"Rennie, I haven't got any other choice."

"Yes, you do. You always have a choice. Just walk away."

"You know I can't do that. It's out of my hands."

Rennie's eyes were filled with tears, and Gray could feel his heart splitting in two.

"Just listen to me for a minute, okay? You don't have to do this. Leave here with me. Now."

"Rennie—"

"The money, the power, whatever they promised you, it's not worth it."

"Honey, stop. I can't—"

"I believe in you, Gray. We can start over, leave L.A. I can help you. All you have to do is agree not to go through with your plans tonight."

Gray couldn't stand to see her so despondent. If things were the way Rennie believed them to be, the choice would have been simple. No amount of money or power would be worth putting Rennie through this kind of torment.

He hated to leave her, but he was running out of time, and TK wasn't likely to be unconscious for much longer.

"I'm sorry, Rennie. I'm so sorry."

"No. Wait—"

Gray bent down to throw TK over his shoulder. "Stay here, Rennie. I'll send someone up to get you when it's safe."

He told himself he had to concentrate on the business at hand. Now that he knew she was safe, he had to complete his mission. Simon would be arriving at any moment—if he wasn't already downstairs waiting for him.

Gray didn't have time to dispose of TK through the proper legal channels, so he locked him in the manager's office. After all the other arrests had been made, they could take TK.

It was quarter past five when Gray finally made it out to the loading dock. His men were unloading the truck.

Flex ran over. "Where have you been, man?"

"I had a few loose ends to attend to. Everything is in order. Are we ready to go?"

"Yeah, we're almost finished unloading the truck."

"Is Simon here?"

"He's right over there."

Gray turned and saw Simon walk out of the back of the truck. A beard covered a good portion of the man's face, but his severe scars were visible. He smiled. Finally this was about to be over.

Once the drugs were in Simon's possession, Gray and his fellow SPEAR agents would take Simon into custody once and for all.

He stretched to shake Simon's hand. "We finally get to meet in person."

Gray's adrenaline shot through the roof as their hands connected. Victory was near. Everything he'd worked for, everything he'd sacrificed would pay off.

Simon kept the handshake brief. He nodded coolly, acknowledging Gray's comment and studying his face. "It seems you've already had an...adventuresome evening?"

Gray reached up to touch the bleeding cut below his eye. "Yes, I'm not afraid to get my hands dirty to protect what's important to me." Suddenly Gray noticed that Simon's left eye was made of glass.

Simon smiled, but only for a few seconds. "Ah, a man after my own heart. We'll work well together."

"That's what I'm counting on."

The guns were stacked along the warehouse floor, and Simon's men were nearly finished loading the drugs onto the truck. Gray readied himself to give the signal.

He couldn't wait to bring Simon to the ground and cuff him.

Suddenly, the warehouse doors burst open and the room flooded with officers. ''Drop your weapons! LAPD!''

''What the—''

''You set me up,'' Simon growled, pulling out a hidden weapon.

Gray's only reply was to leap at Simon, bringing the older man to the ground with him. As the two men struggled, Simon's men, Gray's men, SPEAR agents and police officers launched into a gunfire battle.

Simon managed to break free from Gray as the combat spread into the night-club. In the haze of bloodshed and bullets, it was nearly impossible to know which men were friends and which were foes. Through the chaos, Gray managed to duck the gunfire, tracking Simon as he slipped out the front door of the club.

Gray was only a few seconds behind

him, but he was still too late. He reached
the outside just in time to see Simon grab
onto a suspension rope dangling from a
helicopter that lifted him to safety.

Before Gray could curse his own fail-
ure, a bullet ripped through his flesh.

"I can't believe you're doing this,"
Marlena said, unlocking the passenger
door so Rennie could get out at the cor-
rectional facility.

"I have to. It's my fault that he's here."
When the sound of gunshots and chaos
had subsided, Rennie had ventured down
from the roof. Just in time to see Gray,
wounded in the shoulder, being dragged
away in handcuffs.

Alise leaned forward from the back
seat. "Are you sure you don't want us to
come inside with you?"

"No, I need to do this alone, but thanks
for riding along. I know you both think

I'm crazy, but seeing him here will give me closure.''

Rennie had been haunted by terrible images since she'd seen Gray arrested. She knew he'd been wounded, but she had to see for herself that he was all right.

The guard led her to an empty cubicle, and a few minutes later Gray was brought to her. He looked about as good as she could hope for. His arm was in a cast. There were a few scrapes on his face, but otherwise he appeared to be all right. She was watching for hatred or dismay in his eyes when he saw her. Rennie felt indescribable relief when she didn't see either emotion.

They stared at each other for a few moments before he picked up the phone to speak to her.

''You're the last person I expected to see here.''

''I know, and I must be the last person

you want to see. But I heard that you'd been hurt, and I needed to see for myself that you were…you know, okay.''

''As you can see, I'm fine. What about you? You look like you haven't been getting enough rest. Have you been eating?''

She couldn't believe he was still worrying about her. Of course, she was anything but fine. She was barely sleeping and hardly eating, but there was no sense in telling him that. ''I've been doing as well as can be expected.''

''Well, I'm glad to see you. You're a sight for sore eyes. I want you to know that you did the right thing. I don't blame you for what's happened.''

''How can you say that?''

''Because I know your heart. You wouldn't have made a decision like this easily. I know you weighed the consequences and chose to do what was best. Thank you.''

Rennie couldn't stop the flood of tears that started pouring down her cheeks. This would have been so much easier if he hated her. She'd expected him to tell her that he never wanted to see her again.

More important, she'd been hoping to feel the same way. Despite everything, her mind wouldn't let go of its hope that they would be together. Part of her was hoping that seeing him in prison would wake her from the dream once and for all.

Instead it made her heart ache for things that could never be. She worried over silly things. Would they make sure he got enough to eat? Was he cold at night? Were the beds uncomfortable?

What was she thinking? Prison was supposed to be uncomfortable. It was punishment for his crimes.

"I probably shouldn't stay much longer. My friends are waiting for me in the car. I just wanted to come and tell you that I'm sorry—that I didn't want things to turn out this way. I wished so much better for you.''

Gray lifted a hand to the glass, his eyes filled with emotion. ''I know you did, Rainbow, but I want to tell you something. Come here, look at me.''

Once she'd made eye contact, he continued. ''This isn't your fault. I don't want you to worry about me. We're still connected right here.'' He pointed to his heart. ''No matter what anyone tells you, as long as you can feel me here, I'm okay. Do you understand?''

Rennie took a deep breath, letting her eyes close on the pain washing over her. He was trying to reassure her, but nothing could ease her mind.

''Look at me. Everything's going to be okay. I know you don't believe me, and I'm the last person you want to trust, but it's true.''

''Thank you, but you don't have to be

strong for me. Even behind bars you're trying to protect me.''

''I know it doesn't look this way now, but things can still turn around. You never know which way the wind blows.''

Rennie shook her head. Nothing he was saying made any sense. She wished for once he'd stop trying to be brave and tell her how he really felt. ''Take care of yourself, okay?''

He nodded. ''I realize this may not be worth much to you right now, but I love you, Rennie. I always have and I always will.''

Rennie couldn't take it. She wanted nothing more than to drop dead on the spot. It would be easier than living through the pain and guilt she felt. Coming to see him had been a mistake. Instead of giving her closure, it was opening up old wounds.

She stood. She couldn't think of any parting words that seemed adequate, so she dropped the phone and left.

Chapter 15

Regrets weren't a waste of time, Gray decided. No, he couldn't undo mistakes, but regrets did have a purpose. They allowed him make new and better decisions that might yield fewer regrets down the road.

Prison life the second time around wasn't any better than the first, but it came at a higher price. Rennie. He'd never forget the look in her eyes when she stared at him through the glass wall.

She'd been in her own private world of torture, and no amount of apologies or re-

assurances could free her. At the beginning of his prison term, he'd asked
SPEAR officials if he would finally be
able to let Rennie off the hook and tell her
the truth.

They had denied him permission to
blow his cover, which was in the process
of being reconfigured. He'd been told that
they might need to keep it intact for future
assignments.

Gray had gone along with that decision
at the time. When he'd joined the agency,
they'd asked if he had any assignment
preferences. He'd told them he would go
wherever he was needed and do whatever
he had to, but that had been before he'd
found Rennie again.

Despite all the terrible things she believed about him, she still loved him. She
would never admit it—she had too much
pride for that—but it had been clear. He'd
seen it in the way her lips had tilted into

a shaky smile when their eyes first met, in the way her eyes had filled at the sight of his bandages. And he'd seen it in the way her fingers had massaged that spot over her heart as though she were trying to soothe a very real ache.

He knew just what that ache felt like.

This was all his fault. He should have been stronger. If he'd stayed away from her after that first night at the club, she never would have been hurt by his mission and the lies he'd had to tell her. He'd been selfish, not wanting to deny himself one last chance in her arms.

She'd been in danger, and he couldn't leave her. It was a miracle TK hadn't killed him when he'd had the chance.

He'd made a mess of everything. The LAPD took credit for the bust, reclaiming the weapons Simon planned to exchange. And Simon got away again.

Gray lay back in his bunk, letting his

head sink into the pillow. He was tired. Not just from sleeping with one eye open at night. He was tired of having no roots, no permanent connections. He'd spent his entire life on the move.

Rennie had been right about him all along. He couldn't remember the last time he did something simply because he wanted to. He'd always tried to do what was best for everyone else. This time, by trying to be too many things to too many people, he'd ended up with nothing. It was time to change that.

"Gray." The guard called his name, and he stood as his cell was unlocked. "The warden wants to see you in his office."

The warden excused himself so Gray and Kramer, the official sent from SPEAR, could talk privately.

Kramer sat in the warden's chair and

leaned back. "What's going on, Gray? You said you had something to tell us."

"That's right. I want you to give Jonah a message from me for a change."

"Yeah?"

"I want out."

Kramer sat up straight. "Out of this assignment or out of SPEAR?"

"That depends. I want out of this assignment and any others like it. I want to start having a normal life. I don't have much practice at it, but I'm ready to give it a shot."

Kramer smiled his typically placating smile as he smoothed his hands over his lapels. "Gray, now you know the reason you—"

"Don't even try giving me that crap about my work here being too important. You tell Jonah what I want, or you let me out of the agency completely."

Kramer's lips were tight as he stood,

fastening the buttons on his suit coat. "There's no need to be hostile, Gray. You're one of the best agents in the field. I know you don't want to hear that right now, but you wouldn't have gotten this assignment if you weren't so damn good at what you do."

"Kramer," Gray said with a warning tone.

"Don't get bent out of shape. As much as we hate to lose you in the field, losing you from the organization would be worse."

Gray hadn't realized he had been holding his breath. "Then you'll reassign me?"

"I'm sure we can find you an assignment more suited to a normal life. Just give me forty-eight hours. Then you'll be on your way."

Rennie felt an overwhelming sense of relief after her last client left her office late

Thursday evening. She'd shifted all her appointments so that she could have the Friday before Christmas to enjoy the holidays.

Even if she did pack up a few files to review over the long weekend, it would still be nice not to have to drive to the office for a few days.

Rennie had finished filling her briefcase with paperwork when she heard pounding on the door of her office. She unlocked the door, and Marlena and Alise stumbled in.

Before Rennie could ask what the urgency was about, Alise jerked her into her arms. "Oh, honey, as soon as I heard I called Marlena and we rushed right over."

"Actually," Marlena corrected, "I called Alise. We tried your apartment first. I can't believe you're still trying to work right now."

Rennie pulled away. "What are you

two talking about? What's happened?"
Rennie tried to brace herself for the worst,
but she was unprepared.

Alise's face crumpled. "Oh, my God,
she didn't hear the news?" Tears filled her
eyes, and she was unable to speak.

Rennie's heart rate sped up. "What
news? Somebody tell me what's wrong.
Quickly, before I lose my mind."

Even Marlena, who was always a rock
in times of crisis, had tears in her eyes.
Rennie began to shake.

Marlena took her firmly by the shoulders, looking her directly in the eye.
"Honey, I'm going to give it to you hard
and fast. It's better that way."

Rennie nodded. "Tell me."

"Keshon Gray is dead. He was strangled in his sleep by his cell mate."

Rennie stood blinking at Marlena.
"That's impossible. I just saw him two—
three…how many?" She began to get

hysterical. "Three days ago! I saw him alive on Monday. He's not dead."

Alise tried to pull her into a hug again, but Rennie shook her off. "No. I'll prove it to you. Take me over there. Now! We'll all see that he's alive."

Marlena and Alise were crying right along with her. "Honey, I'm sorry. But he's not. Here, look for yourself." Her friend handed her a newspaper clipping.

Through blurred eyes, Rennie tried to make herself read the words. It was a small paragraph. In the end, that's all his life had warranted. A small paragraph stating that a prisoner by the name of Keshon Gray had been strangled in his sleep.

"Oh, my God. He's really gone."

Rennie unlocked her apartment door, feeling more at loose ends than when she'd left.

Marlena and Alise had meant well when

they'd kidnapped her and taken her to the holiday party a mutual friend was having. It was Christmas Eve, and the two of them couldn't stand the thought of her spending it alone.

Rennie had gone along because she knew if she hadn't they would have spent the evening worrying and calling every other hour.

But as much as she needed their friendship at a time like this, she also needed time alone with her thoughts. Gray was gone—a concept she wasn't able to wrap her mind around.

It was one thing for him to be lost to her because he was in prison. Having him lost to her forever because he was dead...

Rennie felt her knees begin to buckle. Stumbling forward, she managed to catch herself before she could fall.

Unable to handle a fresh wave of mourning, Rennie decided to go to bed.

She dropped her purse on the couch and entered her darkened bedroom, intending to shrug off her clothes and fall straight into bed.

She heard a movement behind her, and suddenly a hand clamped over her mouth. As she struggled in the intruder's solid hold, he dragged her to the doorway and flicked on the light switch.

Without releasing his hold on her mouth, he turned her to face him. Her eyes went wide when she saw that it was Gray. Blinking rapidly, she tried to clear her vision. This had to be an illusion. Gray was dead...wasn't he?

"Sweetheart, can you be quiet and listen?" he asked.

Rennie nodded slowly, and Gray released her. She stumbled backward until she felt the edge of the bed. Shivering, she sank down onto the mattress.

Gray pulled out the chair from her

dressing table and sat in front of her. "Honey, I've been wanting to tell you the truth for so long."

"D-did you break out of prison?"

"No, I didn't."

"But you're alive? I don't understand."

Her eyes drank in the sight of him. She was still too afraid to trust the image she saw before her. In her dreams he was alive, and in waking she lost him all over again. Heaven forbid this was a dream.

As usual, he seemed to read her mind. "It's not a dream, sweetheart." He held out his hand to her. "Touch me. I'm real."

She felt his warm, firm fingers close around hers, and she held on for all she was worth as he spoke.

"That's what I'm trying to explain, Rainbow. I work for a top-secret government agency. The last few months, I was on an undercover assignment trying to track down a traitor to the agency. You sort of got caught in the middle. They faked my death because I told the agency that I wasn't going undercover as a criminal. They gave me a desk job in Washington, D.C.''

Rennie shook her head, trying to take in what he was telling her. ''You work for the government? You're not really in the drug trade or an arms dealer?''

''That's right, Rennie. I'm so sorry that I wasn't able to be honest with you. I was working undercover.''

''Thank God.'' Tears started streaming down Rennie's cheeks. Her trust hadn't been misplaced. Everything she knew in her heart, her gut, her soul about Gray had been true.

''Honey, don't cry. Everything's going to be okay now.'' He reached for her, pulling her onto his lap, rocking her gently. ''I'm being transferred to D.C., and I want you to come with me as my wife. If you're worried about leaving your practice, I'm sure there are plenty of women in need in D.C. I'll help you get started. Whatever you need.''

Rennie leaned forward, giving Gray a long, sweet kiss. ''From now on, where you go, I go. After thinking that I lost you, not once but twice, I'm not letting you out of my sight again.'' She wrapped her arms around him, burying her face in his chest. All she wanted at the moment was to savor his nearness.

''I've been thinking about those things you said to me about living my life for other people,'' Gray whispered into her hair. ''I'm ready to start living my own life. I'm ready to find out who the real Keshon Gray is.''

Rennie raised her head and stared into his eyes. ''I know who he is. He's the man that I love.''

Gray picked her up and flicked off the lights so they could seal their vows in the age-old way of a man and woman in love.

*   *   *   *   *

LARGE PRINT TITLES FOR
JANUARY – JUNE 2005

SPECIAL EDITION™

Sensation™

0105–0605 Silh LP